JOHN CHRISTY EWING, is an accomplished writer, director, Emmy award winning producer, and has appeared as a guest star in L.A. LAW, HILL STREET BLUES, ST. ELSEWHERE, LAW AND ORDER, MURDER SHE WROTE, DALLAS, BARNEY MILLER, and TAXI among many others.

He has also acted major roles in more than two dozen television movies, and has had parts in CLOSE ENCOUNTERS OF THE THIRD KIND, BREAKIN' TWO and MY FAVORITE YEAR.

Prior to his professional acting career in Hollywood, John honed his writing, producing and directing talents as the news director of WDWS the highly successful am and fm Midwestern radio station, as a CLIO AWARD winning producer at the N.W.Ayer advertising agency, as a director with three television commercial production companies, and as an Executive Producer with WBBM- TV Chicago's CBS network station. His work as a writer/ producer for the CBS REPETOIRE WORKSHOP helped the station win an Emmy for that series. He was the Executive Producer of the LEE PHILLIP SHOW, and mainstay of Chicago television. Lee Phillip Bell eventually being of CBS daytime drama fame. He went on to assume writing, producing and directing responsibilities as the Executive Producer for the widely syndicated series Sports Action Pro-File. Prior to returning to an acting career he worked for High Hefner's HMH Publishing as a producer in the Radio, Television and Motion Picture Department.

His theatre credits include in THE CHICAGO CONSPIRACY TRIAL at the Odyssey Theatre and, also at the Odyssey, AT THE BROADWAY CAFÉ WITH SUPERB AND FINE which he wrote, produced, and acted.

For Melissa and Eve.

In loving memory of my daughter Victoria Carey Ewing.

John Christy Ewing

THE RISING TEAR

A CIP catalogue record for this title is available from the British Library.

"ON SUCH A NIGHT AS THIS"
WORDS BY MARSHALL BARER, MUSIC BY HUGH MARTIN
© MORLEY MUSIC CO INC (ASCAP)
ALL RIGHTS ADMINISTERED BY CHAPPELL-MORRIS LTD

ISBN 9781786290977 (Paperback)
ISBN 9781786290984 (Hardback)
ISBN9781786290991 (E-Book)

www.austinmacauley.com

First Published (2016)
Austin Macauley Publishers Ltd.
25 Canada Square
Canary Wharf
London
E14 5LQ

Acknowledgments

Throughout this lengthy process I have been aptly assisted by my friend Marie Tran to whom I am exceedingly grateful.

Vengeance, deep-brooding o'er the slain
Had lock'd the source of softer woe;
And burning pride and high disdain
Forbade the rising tear to flow.

Sir Walter Scott
The Lay of the Last Minstrel

Everyone dies at one time or another.
Just try not to do it before your mother.

Anonymous

Part One

The south side of Chicago in the early 1960's.

"Stop. Before you go any further I need you to answer one question: what is the floor made of?"

"Cement I suppose. I never thought about it, but it would have to be strong, smooth, durable…"

"Of course and the very reason we cannot do your show. Dancers almost always work on wooden floors. Strong, but forgiving. A cement floor could end a dancer's career in one step."

"Of course. Never occurred to me. I understand completely. Well, thank you for agreeing to meet with me. Easily one of the shortest interviews I've ever conducted, however, destined to be one of the most memorable. Have a good run."

After leaving the theatre near the University of Chicago RJ McCaw called his office and was told by his secretary that his college chum and fellow producer Jordan Cahill wanted to meet him at the Chicago Yacht Club where he, Cahill, was a member. RJ, a handsome, but rather unremarkable looking man made a striking contrast to his friend Jordan who was an imposing gentleman who tipped the scale at three hundred and forty pounds and stood tall at six feet eight inches. His friends referred him to as the "mountain that walks like a man."

"I'm sorry I'm late," RJ said. "Traffic was a bitch."

"Isn't it always," Cahill remarked. "No big deal. I had lunch here. Didn't go back to the station."

"I'm surprised you're still mobile."

"Who says I am? I've had to piss for at least an hour, but I was afraid that if I tried to stand I might take a header on the way to the head. How'd it go with Villela?"

"Short and not sweet. Cement floor."

"I wondered about that. Hard on a dancer's legs I would imagine."

"Precisely. Not a total loss, however. I got to watch her and Patricia McBride rehearse for about a half an hour. I'm not nuts about ballet, but those two are really something. So what's going on?"

A waiter comes to the table.

"Good afternoon Mr. Tyler. May I get you something to drink?"

"Yes, please, Tony. The usual. Ah, a double."

"Coming right up."

"So…?"

"I had a meeting this morning with our esteemed leader Michael Haines, Jr. who started off by telling me how much he likes your *Bullish on the Bears* show. Thinks it's shoe-in for a Grammy or two."

"That's nice."

"So, one would imagine. However…"

"I've got a feeling I'm not going to like this."

"Precisely. In his next breath he informs me that you are going to be fired."

"What! You can't be serious."

"I know it is rare, however, unfortunately, this is one of those times."

"I don't get it. What have a done? Did he say?"

"No. In point of fact he intimated that the word had come from on high. He didn't clarify. He seemed very ill at ease with the whole business. We both know he's a snake, but I sensed that this was different. That it was a decision he hadn't made and that he was very uncomfortable with. Pressure from New York maybe. He didn't say. Maybe somebody's kid needs a job. I did. My father made a phone call. So it wouldn't be the first time."

"I'm stunned."

"I know. So am I. Look, I got a call last week from Bob Greene. You don't know him. He's our affiliate station manager in Miami. He worked here for a while in radio. He's desperate for a writer/director to do feature pieces and docs for their sports department. He just happened to ask, jokingly, if you were available. He evidently knows your work."

"I don't know. Jesus, Miami. Then again Ginny's father lives there in one of his many houses. She adores him although why escapes me. A prick with ears."

"Speaking of which, how are things going on the home front?"

"Still rocky. I can't seem to do anything right."

When RJ got to the studio the security guard informed him that he was to report to Mr. Haines' office immediately. Instead RJ stopped by his office to check in with his secretary who was not there. She had left a note on his desk that read: That cock sucker Haines fired me this morning without any explanation other than "my position was being terminated since you were also leaving." We're both better off outa' here. Love you. Fay.

RJ walked into Haines' office without knocking and left the door open. Haines' desk was elevated. Not much. Just enough to lord him over whomever was sitting across from him. Everyone except Cahill, who at six feet eight inches was always eye-to-eye with him.

Jordan maintained that he could ascertain a slight tick in Haines' right eye that Jordan was sure was due to his being on equal footing as it were. Haines has his back to the door and is looking at eight TV monitors that show all the stations in the area. He does not immediately acknowledge RJ.

Finally.

"You didn't knock."

"Right. Since it seems I'm leaving ignoring protocol didn't seem terribly important under the circumstances."

"Sit down."

"I'd rather stand. I get the feeling this is going to be a short meeting."

"Anyone ever tell you, you have a real arrogant streak?"

"Constantly. One of my better characteristics."

Haines opens a file.

"When we have our by monthly meeting to discuss upcoming guests on the Mid-Day in Chicago show I thought you understood that if I nixed a possible guest that was it. End of story."

RJ doesn't reply nor does his face show any reaction.

"Well? Do you have anything to say?"

"I'm sorry. Was there a question there?" "I guess it depends on who you or what you're upset about."

"Let's start with the blind guy and his dog. Why the dog?"

"His name, the singer, is Jose Feliciano. He's very hot now. We're lucky to get him. Being blind he doesn't go anywhere without his dog. They're buddies."

"I also say no to what's her name… King."

"Coretta Scott King the wife of Martin Luther King. What's wrong with having her on? I got her. No other show did."

"Too controversial."

"Controversial! Her husband is a noble Peace Prize winner!"

Just then an attractive, sexy, young, blonde girl comes bouncing into the office. She is one of RJ's assistants. RJ has been pacing the room and she doesn't immediately see him.

"You 'bout ready to go, hon?"

Then she sees RJ.

"Oh, hi, RJ."

"Sally? Oh, shit! I got it. You're boffing Haines so that you can get my job. Great deal for him. A nice young piece of ass that makes less than half of what I do…excuse me…did."

"Hold it right there, RJ. I can see how this looks, but…"

"You can? Okay, tell me. I'm curious, just how does it look?"

Sally has burst into tears and heads for the door.

"Stay here. I was just leaving. Permanently."

RJ starts to leave and then changes his mind and grabs an Emmy off the trophy shelf.

"I wrote this one."

Then he picks up two more.

"And I wrote and produced both of these. I guess that about does it."

"Just wait a minute. You can't…I'm calling security.

Fine. Call 'em. And while you're doing that I'll call your wife. Wait a minute…what do I want with this worthless shit."

He returns one of the statues slamming it down and shattering the glass shelf in the process. Next he takes the other two and throws them up against the wall of monitors breaking two in the process.

"Whoops!"

Just then a security guard comes rushing in.

"GET THIS MANIAC OUT OF MY OFFICE!"

Driving home RJ thought that this was the worst day of his life. He couldn't imagine anything worse happening to him until he walked through the front and heard his wife screaming from the kitchen with a shriek that could shatter glass.

18

"Where the fuck have you been? Do you know what time it is?"

RJ put down his coat and bag and with some trepidation entered the kitchen. The first thing he noticed was that Ginny, his forty something knockout wife had a drink in one hand and a cigarette in the other. He walked over to his daughter who was being fed by the baby sitter.

"I'm sorry I'm late. I stopped off for a drink with some of the guys. It's Cookie Gaspadarek's birthday."

"Whoever the fuck that is."

"Would you please watch you language."

"I'm not a baby, Daddy."

"You know we were supposed to be at the Mechling's twenty minutes ago."

"Oh, god, I forgot all about it. I'm sorry. I'll take a shower and get dressed. Give me fifteen minutes."

"You can't find your putz in fifteen minutes. We'll take both cars. I'll see you when you get there."

"Do we have to go? I was kinda' hoping we could spend the evening together. Just the three of us."

"Ginny gives RJ a look that says the question doesn't even deserve a reply."

"Sweet. A little late, but a nice idea."

She puts out her cigarette in a dinner plate and chugs the rest of her drink. Pats RJ on the cheek, kisses Callie, grabs her purse, keys, a gaily wrapped package off the counter, and heads for the back door.

"Remember it's Bud's birthday and it's black tie. I picked up your tux shirt at the cleaners. It's hanging on the closet door. Try to get your fingernails clean: it's a sit down dinner."

"Ginny ..."

"What?"

"Nothing… just I love you, that's all. I'll see you in a few minutes."

"Gin…"

But she has gone. RJ looks at his nails. They're clean. RJ starts for the bedroom and abruptly changes his mind. He sprints for the front door. Ginny is pulling out of the driveway.

"Ginny!"

"What?"

"I… I got fired today."

"You're kidding."

"Does this sound like a joke?"

"Christ. What are you going to do?"

"I don't know."

"Great. Just fucking great."

And with that she peels away.

RJ wanders back into the kitchen. Callie and the baby sitter aren't there. He can hear them laughing in the bathroom as the tub is filling. He makes himself a large scotch and water and heads upstairs for the shower. A short time later freshly shaved, showered, and wrapped in a towel he's back in the kitchen replenishing his drink. On the rocks this time. RJ walks from the kitchen to the bedroom passing through the living room where the kids are watching TV. Back in the bedroom he tears the cleaner's wrapper off the shirt only to discover that it is way too small and that it is light blue with a stripe.

"Jesus Christ! This isn't my shirt."

RJ throws the shirt, opens the closet door and frantically looks for a shirt he can wear. Lots of shirts. Not one white one.

"Fuck!"

In the far corner of the closet hangs something RJ can't seem to place. As he removes it from the closet he reads the card that falls to the floor. 'Happy Birthday to our sweet RJ from Aunt Dort and Uncle John.' In a suit bag he discovers a sheik's outfit. On the floor of the closet he finds a pair of bright red shoes with turned up toes and tries them on.

"Perfect. Perfect. Perfect."

RJ takes a big slug of his drink and starts rummaging around on the top shelf of the closet and finds what he has been looking for: a small black case containing theatrical makeup.

"Ginny, my darling, I don't know why you saved this, but I'm glad you did."

Callie and the sitter look away from the television set as this strangely attired guy darts through the living room in the direction of the kitchen. RJ pours a fresh drink into a large plastic mug with a Chicago Bears logo emblazoned on it. RJ bolts half way out the back door with drink in hand. He stops, turns back and puts on his sunglasses even though it is dark outside. He catches his image in the window of the back door and arches a false, bushy eyebrow at his new self.

"Okay, Omar, let's boogie."

RJ's car turns off the street of the very upscale neighborhood onto the circular driveway narrowly missing the mailbox. The street is full of parked cars and a handwritten sign asks guests to leave the driveway clear for departing guests as rain is expected. Having read the sign RJ drives past the entrance to the house and having missed the turn comes to a halt on the lawn. RJ emerges in full regalia. He checks his appearance in the exterior rear-view mirror and, receiving his own approval, heads for the front door somewhat unsteadily.

RJ enters the Mechling's foyer, which holds several groups of people, drinks and hors d'oeuvres in hand. The guests seem puzzled: who can this guy be? A client of the host, perhaps? RJ nods to one of the groups and moves through the living room. A waiter with a tray full of drinks passes near enough for RJ to stop him and commandeer one of the drinks: a straight up Martini. RJ takes a large sip, shudders, and moves towards the veranda of the house where a small combo is playing. There is a small dance floor and tables are set under umbrellas. The swimming pool is awash with flowers. RJ looks around trying to spot Ginny. An attractive fiftyish woman approaches him. Our hostess. She is trying to determine, since it's not a costume party, why this man is dressed the way he is.

"I'm sorry; I don't believe we've met. I'm…"

"I know who you are, Jane, and you've known me for most of my life."

"That voice. I know that voice from some … RJ? RJ, is that you?"

Another waiter carrying a drink-laden tray passes by and RJ stops him while polishing off his drink and exchanges it for a fresh one while scanning the guests trying to locate Ginny.

"The very same. Lovely party. Have you seen the Gin?"

"I saw her a moment ago near the bar by the pool. She was talking to Karl Hoff."

"What's that Nazi doing back in town? Looking for a rich, helpless widow, no doubt."

"Now you behave yourself. Do not…let me repeat myself…do not make a scene. And he is not a Nazi. He's not even German, for God's sake. He's from somewhere in Scandinavia, I believe."

"Via Argentina or Chile, I'll bet. I'm going to find Ginny. See you later."

"What does she think about your little… costume?"

"She doesn't know about it. My idea."

"Oh, dear."

RJ starts to mingle. He sidles up to an attractive young woman and sings.

I'm the Sheik of Araby... with no pants on... your love belongs to me... with no pants on. At night when you're asleep...with no pants on...

The man with the young woman has had enough.

"Hey, piss off asshole."

"Anything you say, effendi. No need to be offendi, effendi."

Ginny and a tall blond Nordic man, Karl Hoff, are engaged in intimate conversation. It is obvious that the man has something of a sexual proposal in mind and Ginny does not seem totally averse to the idea. She sees RJ approaching but doesn't immediately recognize him. RJ stops at the bar for a fresh drink. Just what he needs at this point. Ginny catches on.

"Oh, Jesus."

"Ginny, what is it? Are you all right?"

"I'm fine, Kurt. Would you excuse me for a moment? I have to strangle someone."

We leave Kurt somewhat puzzled, but he is a worldly chap and recovers easily as an unattended seventy-year-old dowager passes by.

RJ is standing by the bar rather amusedly watching Ginny approach. He may find the situation mildly hilarious, but he also knows he's in big trouble. Ginny is waylaid on her way to RJ by her mother Helena, and her stepfather Henry a very attractive seventyish couple.

"Ginny, dear, is that who I think it is?"

"I'm going to kill him. I'm really going to kill him. Would you excuse me?"

RJ realizes he is standing next to Bob Mechling, the host of the party. Mechling is talking with a dark-complexioned, distinguished looking man with a mustache and goatee.

"Hey, Bud; I didn't notice you standing there. How're ya' doin'?"

Bud does not immediately recognize the speaker. When he does he is mildly horrified.

"Oh, hello, RJ how are you?"

"Great. Just great. Who's your friend?"

Before Mechling can react RJ says, "Hi, I'm RJ McCaw. How are ya'?"

"RJ, this is Sheik Muhammed al Hareem. The Sheik is the Saudi Ambassador to the United States. We were roommates at Harvard."

"Harvard. Really. Fight fiercely, fellows, cocktails at seven. Remember that one?"

Blank stares from both men.

"And you came all the way from Africa for the party. What a guy."

"Actually, I was in New York. The Assembly is in session now."

"Is that a fact? What do you know, Joe? You chaps want a drink?"

RJ has not noticed Ginny approaching.

"Well, if it isn't Omar the tent maker. What are you doing in town, Omar? Come in for the camel races did you? Can I have a few words with you sweetie? Excuse us will you, Bob? Mr. Ambassador. What the fuck do you think you're doing, you dick head? Are you trying to embarrass me in front of my friends or…"

"Hey, I…"

"Shut up. Just shut the fuck up."

And now others, including Ginny's mother and stepfather, have started to watch the confrontation. One of the men mouths "Who is that?"

"Keep a wrinkle in it, will you, Gin. Let's get a drink. I see the Kraut is sniffin' around. Rekindling the old flame are we?"

Ginny pinches the underside of his bicep.

"Ow! Dammit, that hurt."

"Really?"

"It's a joke. Big deal. I thought it would be funny … you know… What's the problem anyway?"

"The problem? I'll tell you what the problem is. You're the goddamn problem, that's what the problem is. How long are you going to keep up this … this masquerade?"

"As a matter of fact I'm thinking of leaving right now. I'm suddenly not feeling too well."

"Going to be sick? Why not? You make me sick. So I'm not surprised."

And with that admission RJ quickly turns, knocking over a waiter with a tray of drinks and hastily makes his way through the guests towards what he hopes is the front door. RJ exits the house and gulps a huge breath of air. He looks around as if to remember where he parked his car and cannot, even though the car is on the lawn just a few feet to his right. He teeters down the sidewalk in the other direction.

"Air. Gotta' have air."

RJ works his way down the line of parked cars. Focusing is a problem he tries to solve by covering one eye with his hand and grasping his dark glasses with the other. Eventually he comes to the end of the line of cars without discovering his. What to do? If he could just lie down for a moment he would feel a lot better. RJ approaches a large house on a slight incline. The yard is covered with gorgeous, soft, lush grass. The perfect spot for a short rest. RJ lies down on his back and immediately passes out. A short time later although his face is fully illuminated, RJ is still asleep. The owners of the house where our hero is resting have returned from a night out and seeing an Arab spread eagled on their lawn have turned on the exterior light fully illuminating the scene. Six or eight couples from the Mechling party are assembled on the sidewalk wondering what, if anything, to do. Standing, by the way, under umbrellas for it has started to rain. The couple in the house can be seen talking on the telephone. The man of the house is apparently shouting something to the person on the other end of the line, waving his hand and pointing at RJ.

The rain is having its effect now. The dark pancake makeup is running and the fake mustache is listing hard to starboard. One false eyebrow is among the missing. Suddenly RJ's face is illuminated from the beam of a strong flashlight causing RJ to shield his eyes and at the same time trying to see the cop holding the flashlight just as he passes out for good this time.

The next morning a cab pulls up in front of the McCaw house. RJ looking much the worse for the trauma of the previous evening and a night spent in jail gets out, pays the cabbie, and sheepishly enters the house. In the kitchen Ginny is feeding Callie.

"Daddy!"

"Well if it isn't the poor man's Peter O'Toole. You don't look so good, Lawrence. Have a nice night in the slammer did we?"

"Lovely. Thanks for bailing me out."

"Believe it or not I tried. No go. The cop said you'd have to be arraigned before bail was set and that wouldn't happen until this morning. Nothing I could do."

"The judge let me off with a warning. He's a friend of my father's."

"Lucky for you. You want some coffee?"

"Later. Think I'll take a shower first. Maybe try to get some sleep."

"Not likely, Omar. I'm playing tennis and then lunch with the girls. You and her nibs are spending the day together."

Callie claps her hands.

"Yeah!"

RJ holds his head.

RJ and Callie do in fact have a day. After some breakfast and a gallon of coffee RJ gets Callie dressed and they head off in his car. RJ, rightly, has figured that a lot of fresh air might be the best thing for his head and he has put the top down on the car. Raggedy Ann is along for the ride. Callie won't go anywhere without her doll. Or as she calls her, "My bestest friend."

Walking along Lake Michigan. Lying down looking up at the clouds. The mandatory swings and then eating dinner together in a kid friendly restaurant called Andy's where there is a larger than life Raggedy Andy doll. Riding home in the car with the top up Callie is asleep with the doll in the back seat. RJ puts Callie to bed propping up Raggedy Ann beside her. RJ walks out onto the front porch where Ginny is putting books in boxes and placing them next to the pile that contains suitcases, golf clubs, etc.

"What's going on?"

"I'm packing your stuff. What's it look like?"

"I don't understand…"

"No surprise there. I didn't play tennis. I spent a few hours with an attorney instead."

"An attorney? I don't…"

Ginny finishes with the box and wipes a lock of hair out of her eye.

RJ, I'm going to tell you a joke. Listen carefully. A woman comes home and yells to her husband who is upstairs. RJ, pack your bags. I just won the lottery. Husband RJ comes running down the stairs. What shall I pack? Will it be hot? Will it be cold? I don't give a good goddamn, says the wife. I just want you the fuck out of here.

RJ who is not only shocked and befuddled but visibly on the verge of totally coming undone.

Sometime later RJ and friend Jordan are sailing on Jordan's forty-foot sloop. They are finishing trimming the sails and are having a wonderful day. Jordan pops a couple of beers.

"So, how are things on the home front?"

"Just about as bad as they can be. Ginny's put the house on the market and I have to be out by the end of the week. Until that time I'm the invisible man."

I notice you don't say "our house."

"Very observant, old boy. It seems that since Dorsey, Ginny's terribly charming father, put the house in Ginny's name only. He also paid the down payment and the first two years of the monthlies. So the house lock, stock, and barrel is hers. How' bout them apples?"

"So, where are you going to live?"

"No idea. Nor, as you are aware, do I have a job. Other than that things are just jolly."

"Look, I have plenty of room and you can stay there as long as you like."

"Thank you. I just might take you up on that."

"How did Ginny react when you told her you were fired?"

"In a word...she went ballistic. Tomorrow we meet with her lawyer."

"Who has she hired?"

"Lou Gottlieb."

"Christ...the Executioner. And you. Who do you have?"

"Me."

"You? You don't have a lawyer."

"Can't afford one. Pure and simple."

RJ and Ginny are sitting across from Lou Gottlieb a large man in a three-piece lawyer suit.

RJ, there are a number of things we need to discuss today. I understand you don't feel the need to be represented by counsel?

Not right now. I can't really afford one. At the moment I'm unemployed.

"Unemployed? What happened?"

"I got fired. Simple as that."

"I'm sorry to hear that, RJ."

"But I have some possibilities lined up."

"Well, good luck finding something."

"Thank you, Counsellor."

"So, let's move on. At this moment in time it's difficult to get a divorce in this state simply because the two parties can't get along. Therefore, our options are rather limited. Physical cruelty or adultery. That's about it. It is Ginny's opinion, and I agree with her, that physical cruelty is the only viable option."

"A wife beater? Not on your life. My parents live in this town."

"RJ, let me explain, this is the way it's done. It's strictly a formality. Everyone knows that, even the judge."

"I don't like it. I don't like it a lot."

RJ gets up and walks to the window. He knows he doesn't have much of a chance of winning this argument.

"I'll tell you what. I'll go along with adultery."

Ginny and Gottlieb look at each other. Is he kidding?

"You won't go along with physical cruelty because of what people might think of you, but you will go along with adultery?"

"Look all I'm saying is I don't beat up women they just like me."

RJ is rather proud of himself. Ginny, on the other hand, is convinced that this is just one more example of what a loser RJ is. Gottlieb doesn't know whether to take RJ seriously or not.

RJ follows Ginny, who is hurrying to get away from him, to the office parking lot.

"Women just like me. Jesus Christ RJ, where the fuck do you get that shit?"

"That must be a record: Jesus Christ, shit and fuck all in one short sentence. Amazing."

They hurry along in silence. Ginny sets a breakneck pace.

"Are we late for something?"

"We? You know I'm trying to remember what it was I saw in you."

"Try real hard."

"I am and it's not working."

"Maybe I reminded you of your first husband, what's his name, the ski instructor."

"Twice the man you ever were."

"Which is why he left you when you were seven months pregnant with Chase and ran off to Mexico with … what was it you called her … oh, yeah… a two buck hooker with a million dollar overbite."

"Look asshole, I've had it with you. Just get the fuck out of my life."

"Not that easy. I plan on being a part of my daughter's life and that's something you can't control."

"Really? We'll see about that. You'll get to see Callie when it's good and goddamn convenient for me and don't think for one minute I'm going to make it easy for you. Have a gray day, dick-head."

As Ginny heads for a new, white, Cadillac convertible parked in the law office parking lot, her father, Dorsey, a handsome man in his mid-sixties, gets out of the driver's side and opens the passenger door for her.

"Hello, RJ, how are you?"

"Wonderful, Dorsey. Couldn't be better."

"Sorry to hear that."

"I'm sure."

"Oh," Ginny says, "I almost forgot. Callie made this for you."

Ginny hands RJ a crude, but very cute, drawing of a man holding hands with a little girl who is clutching a Raggedy Ann doll. "I love you Daddy" is scrawled across the bottom. An unstoppable sadness engulfs RJ and his eyes fill with tears. Ginny grabs the drawing from RJ and tears it into a number of pieces and throws them in RJ's direction.

"Charming girl, your daughter. Takes after you does she?"

"You know, RJ, I never liked you, and now that you and Ginny are no longer an item, I think I just might do something about it."

"Ooh, ooh, please Mr. Man don't hurt me."

Dorsey starts to punch RJ, thinks better of it, gets into the car, and drives off narrowly missing RJ in the process. Ginny gives RJ the finger.

"Like I said... charming."

RJ retrieves the pieces of the torn drawing.

Suddenly the Cadillac backs up and stops next to RJ.

"One more thing: I was going to tell you this later but why wait. Callie and I are leaving tomorrow for Florida. Daddy's has found a house for us. Here's the address. Since you don't have a lawyer, at this point, perhaps we can settle this whole thing out or court, or so Lou tells me, without either of us having to appear in court. Any comment?"

"No, I guess not."

"Come on Daddy; let's get the fuck out of here."

A brilliant day on Lake Michigan A strong, but manageable wind, perfect for sailing. Jordan's boat is an older, beautifully maintained, wooden-hulled sloop rigged beauty from the pre-World War Two era. RJ is at the wheel. Jordan is handling lunch and drinks from the below deck galley.

"What do you want to drink?"

"Just a beer. What a great day! I'm really love this boat. Someday I'm going to have one just like it."

"Save your pennies. You know they have sailboats in Florida."

"Really. Is that a fact?"

"I've heard tell. Maybe it's just a rumor."

They sail on eating and drinking. Enjoying the day and each other's company. Who knows when they'll see each other again?

"What do you hear from your soon to be ex?"

"Not much. Her father got them a house with a pool in Boca Raton. Callie's been enrolled in a private school. That's about it."

"What's your plan…work wise?"

"I called that guy you mentioned…the one in Miami. He wants me to come down for, as he put it, a chat."

"And….?"

"He sounded pretty positive about hiring me. I guess I'll do it. I'm thinking about driving down. I don't have that much stuff. Load up the car and head down. I could sure stand a change of scenery. Seems like whenever I turn around I see something that reminds me of Ginny and Callie."

"What's the state of affairs between you and Ginny?"

"Good question. Wish I had a good answer. Probably find out once I get there."

RJ pulls off highway I-95 at one of the Fort Lauderdale exits and begins looking for a place to stay. They all seem pretty much the same. The he spots a sign reading THE OCEAN RAN HOTEL FORT LAUDERDALE'S FINEST. A smaller sign reads vacancy. RJ wonders what Ocean Ran means.

RJ says to himself, "And it has a Tiki Bar...whatever that is."

RJ pulls into a parking space and heads for the front desk. A sign above the main entrance to the hotel states: THE OCEAN RANCH HOTEL. How bad can it be?

The next morning RJ has slept late. He looks around his room. Not bad. Not bad at all. Ground floor room that looks out onto the ocean. Quite nice actually. He does a quick unpack, pulls on a pair of shorts, top-siders, a polo shirt, and after reading a sign in the lobby advertising breakfast after eleven at the Tiki Bar, heads for the beach.

A woman's volleyball tournament is in full swing. Banners advertising the sponsorship by Bacardi Rum are strewn from the thatched roof hut. The bar is crowded with mostly young men and women in their late twenties and early thirties. As RJ looks for a place to sit one of the games ends and two people vacate their seats at the bar. A bartender approaches.

"How ya' doin'?"

"Great! Is it too late for a little coffee?"

"Not at all. I've got freshly brewed coffee … a house specialty… freshly squeezed orange juice, and I think I've still got one croissant."

"Also fresh?"

"Absolutely."

"Sounds great. I'll have all of the above."

"Cream and sugar?"

"Neither, thanks. Black."

"Comin' up."

"Say, could I also have a rum and Coke? After the coffee, etcetera."

"Absolutely."

RJ swivels his bar stool around and watches the new match getting under way. He is vaguely aware of a new presence. A man of indeterminate age has seated himself next to RJ. The bartender returns with RJ's breakfast. The stranger sitting next to RJ speaks with a slight British accent.

"Cuba Libre."

"What's that?"

"That's what it's called. Your drink. A Cuba Libre. Rum and Coke."

"Yes, I know."

"But you were embarrassed to order it that way. Thought it might sound pretentious."

"Yeah, maybe"

"Not down here. Lots of Cubans in South Florida."

"So I've heard."

"They'll own the whole dammed state soon enough."

"Is that right?"

"Damn straight. We'll all be eatin' nothin' but black beans and rice. Mark my words."

RJ takes in this character. He needs a shave and though he doesn't look dirty there is a slight seedy quality about him. He might be fifty. He might be older. It's impossible to tell. He wears old chinos, an even older Hawaiian shirt, and an archaic pair of topsiders with a toe or two showing that make RJ's look brand new by comparison, and a battered Panama hat.

RJ looks around the bar for another place to sit.

"You won't find one."

"What's that?"

"Another place to sit. We're lucky we got these. Usually this place fills up and stays that way all day when there's a tournament. I come every time there's a ladies' tournament. Wouldn't miss the action for the world."

He winks at RJ, chortles a bit at his own mischievousness, and in the process has a minor coughing fit.

"Dammit!"

He takes a battered pack of Camels out of his pocket, offers one to RJ, who refuses and lights one up.

"I have hundreds of times."

"Tried to quit?"

"Right."

"Names MacDivitt. Capital D. Two t's. Harry MacDivitt."

Harry offers his hand, which RJ takes rather gingerly. After they shake RJ wants to check his hand for dirt, but manages to resist the impulse.

"You a guest of the hotel?"

"Yeah."

"I didn't get your name."

"RJ. RJ McCaw."

RJ figures if he ignores this guy maybe he'll disappear.

"So what brings you to these parts? Volleyball?"

"Volleyball?"

"The tournament."

"No. I... I'm interviewing for a job in Miami."

"Really. What do you do?"

"I work in television... Chicago. I'm a writer/producer."

"So, what do you write/produce?"

Wise guy. Harry couldn't be less interested. He appears to be torn between checking out the bar and falling asleep.

"All sorts of things. The Miami job is in the news and documentary department."

"You don't say."

Harry lights another cigarette from the stub of the one he is already smoking and has another coughing fit. This one is much worse than the first causing his eyes to water and other patrons to consider moving away from him, but, as he has said, there are no other places. The bar area slowly begins to darken as if a fast moving cloud is directly overhead. We hear the sound of a motor. A sound similar to an airplane, but softer.

Harry jumps off his stool almost falling over.

"It's the blimp! It's that god dammed flying piece of shit again!"

Harry half runs and half falls onto the playing field, his arms waving fiercely in the air, cursing the Bacardi logoed ship, hacking from the cigarettes, and, in the process, losing a shoe. The sand is very hot by this time of day and contributes to Harry's eventually losing his balance as he runs into a volleyball game. "Go back to Ohio or wherever the hell you came from."

One of the other spectators at the bar recognizes Harry.

"That's the tire company, Harry. Wrong blimp!"

Harry has now become disoriented from the exertion, the hacking, looking into the sun for the airship, and runs pell-mell into the net and falls down, his hat over his eyes. RJ puts some money on the bar and beats a hasty retreat.

MIAMI. SOUTH EAST TELEVISION INTERNATIONAL

A uniformed security guard is behind the reception desk. RJ is seated scanning a magazine when Bob Greene, a tall, athletic man in a shirt and tie enters the reception area and crosses to RJ. Greene has a concerned look on his face.

"RJ?"

RJ stands and the two shake hands.

"Bob Greene. I've been trying for two days to get a hold of you, but nobody in Chicago seemed to know where you were."

"Well, you know how it is once you leave Big Brother… you kinda' feel like a pariah."

"I know what you mean. I wanted to tell you that the position we wanted to talk to you about has already been filled. It was one of those political things that happen once in a while. Totally out of my control."

"I'm really sorry about this, RJ, you're coming all this way."

"That's okay. Worse places to be than Florida at this time of the year."

"Right. Well, I don't know what to say. What do you think you'll do?"

From the look on RJ's face it is obvious he hasn't a clue.

The next day RJ is having breakfast in the Ocean Ranch coffee shop. The Miami Herald want ads are spread out on the table. He has a Magic Marker and several area maps of Fort Lauderdale, Miami, etc. He does a lot of looking. Little marking. He circles one ad that promises pleasant working conditions and up to ten thousand dollars a month.

Later that same day RJ enters a boiler room. Lots of desks and phones. A coffee machine in one corner and lots of smoke. RJ is approached by a tough looking guy with the stub of a cigar in his month. RJ makes an instant decision and backs out the door.

The Fort Lauderdale Marina. RJ is walking along the boardwalk, which parallels one of the boat yards. A sailboat catches his eye and he walks toward it. He checks it out from bow to stern.

"Real salty, isn't she?"

RJ turns to see a large man in a shiny suit with a large un-lit cigar and dark glasses smiling at him.

"Yeah, nice. Chris Craft. The power boat people."

"Not a lot of people know they also made sailboats."

"Used to be one of these in Chicago, Belmont Harbor. Some guy from Playboy owned it. I drooled every time I saw it."

"You lookin' to buy a yacht?"

"No, actually I just interviewed for a job with your competition."

"What kind of a job? Salesman?"

"Yeah."

"Which one?"

"I'd rather not say."

"Short, wiry guy? Couldn't seem to stand still?"

"Ah, yeah, that's him. How'd you know?"

"That jerk can't keep help. He screws his own guys worse than his customers. Where you from?"

"Chicago."

"You sail?"

"Yeah."

"Where?"

"Lake Geneva... Wisconsin. Great Lakes."

"What kinda' boats?"

"Everything from day sailers to fifty, sixty feet."

"Maybe we should talk. I'm just goin' out for a sandwich. You had lunch?"

"Ah, no."

"Great. Hang on a sec. I wanna' tell my secretary where I'm goin'."

"You work here?"

"Are you kiddin'? Pointing to a sign. King Yachts. That's me, Frankie King. I own the joint. Come on, I'll give you the twenty-five cent tour, after we can catch a bite."

Frankie and RJ are seated at a table underneath an umbrella overlooking another boat yard and the docking area of the restaurant. While they lunch several Cigarette boats arrive and depart. They are all driven by young men who seem to be on top of the world. Lots of pretty women along for the ride. A very sexy waitress brings them drinks.

"Thanks, sweetheart. How about that?"

"Not bad."

"Yeah, right. Not bad. Ha."

The boys sip their drinks and watch a yacht sail by.

"You married?"

"What time is it?"

"Sorry. Me too. Several times. You got any kids?"

"A daughter. You?"

"Are you kidding? I'm on my fourth. The only thing the other three knew how to do was fuck and call a lawyer."

"Gets expensive."

"Enough said."

Frankie lights a cigar and hails the waitress.

"Sweetheart, do you think you can get us a couple more of these and some menus?"

"Right away, Mr. King."

"Thanks… (trying to read her name tag) Annabelle."

She smiles at Frankie and exits the scene. Frankie watches her leave.

"That girl scares me to death and I'm fearless. You know about sail boats … what about powerboats?"

"Ah, not much. Not my style."

Frankie thinks for a moment.

"No matter. When could you start?"

"You offering me a job?"

"That's what I like about you, RJ, you're quick. Commission against an advance. You get a check every week whether you sell anything or not. Same arrangement as all my guys. What do you say? Deal?"

"RJ is clearly elated."

"Yeah, why not? Deal."

Frankie grasps RJ's hand in both of his. A handshake to seal the deal. Frankie shouts, "Annabelle, I'm getting awfully thirsty."

A small public parking lot on the street side of the Intracoastal Highway. RJ is sitting in his parked car drinking a beer. His attention is on the back yard of a tasty Spanish style home painted a subtle pink. There is an illuminated swimming pool. From what RJ can see through the foliage the property is lovely and well lit. After a short time a door opens and Ginny comes out of the house with a drink and a cigarette in one hand and a cordless phone in the other. She manages to balance all three. She walks around to the opposite side of the pool and stands staring across the water; it appears she is looking right at RJ. He slides down in the seat of his car even though he's fairly certain she can't see him. After a while she hangs up the phone just as Dorsey enters from the house. He is very irritated about something. He and Ginny start a heated argument. RJ strains to hear what they are saying, but a passing yacht obliterates their conversation. As the boat passes Dorsey throws up his hands in disgust and re-enters the house. Ginny slugs her drink, flips her cigarette into the canal, and stands staring in RJ's direction. RJ finds himself thinking: Ah, the father and daughter relationship. What a wonderful thing.

Later that same evening as RJ enters the mostly empty Tiki Bar he sees Harry just as Harry sees him and motions him over.

"RJ!"

Too late to escape. RJ resigns himself to the situation. Besides he'd prefer not to be alone this evening. How bad can it be?

"Hi ... Harry?"

"Indeed. Nice of you to remember. The last time we met I ... well, let's just say...."

"Hey, forget it. No big deal. Can I buy you a drink?"

"My treat. Tender of the bar, a little service, if we may. So, laddie, how was your day? I seem to remember something about your having a job interview today. Television, wasn't it?"

"Ah, it didn't work out."

The evening shift bartender approaches.

"Gentleman, what can I get you?"

"A Bacardi Anejo on the rocks with a squeeze of lime ... better make that a double ... save you a trip, and a Cuba Libre for my friend?"

"You don't forget a thing do you, Harry? I'll have the same thing he's having … whatever it is."

"So, what have you been up to?"

"Well, I did get a job. Not in television though."

"Indeed? Will wonders never cease. Doing what, pray tell?"

"Selling boats."

"That's a switch. For whom?"

"King Yachts in the Lauderdale marina. You heard of them?"

"Oh, yes. It is virtually impossible to live in South Florida and not to have heard of Frankie King. A minor legend in these parts."

"I got an apartment, too. Move in over the weekend."

"You have been busy. Where?"

"Just off Broward."

"Broward? Is it safe?"

"Of course it's safe. Sorta'."

"Sorta'?"

"Well, the neighborhood is … what's it called… sociologically transitional."

"I beg your pardon?"

"I read that once … in a magazine."

The next day RJ is on an indoctrination tour with Frankie along the rows of boats. Frankie pointing out various aspects of each craft: below decks looking at a large diesel engine, in the cockpit of a power yacht examining the Loran navigation system, in the office going over contracts with the office manager.

Later RJ is showing a yacht to a slightly balding male customer and his companion; a rather plain-faced young woman, with a spectacular body, who seems uninterested in the boat until they enter the Captain's sleeping quarters, where she leaps onto the king sized round bed. Eventually the couple is being escorted out of the boat yard. RJ hands the man his business card.

Towards the end of the day RJ and Frankie are seated in the sales office.

"So, didja' learn anything today?"

"Yeah, never believe a guy who asks for your card and says he'll think about it and call you tomorrow."

"Very good. Spot on. Unfortunately, I know this guy. Comes in once ... twice a year ... whenever he has a new bimbo on the line and wants to get laid. Never even buys a pair of topsiders. You want to catch some dinner? My wife's out for the evening with her girlfriends. Some fag musical."

"Thanks, but I'm beat. Not used to the heat. Think I'll grab a sandwich and turn in early."

Later that evening RJ is once again parked in his spot in the parking lot across the causeway from Ginny's house. The scene is much the same as before. However this time RJ is perusing the house through binoculars. No sign of life. The house is dimly lit. The only illumination outside is in the swimming pool. RJ is eating a hamburger with fries and a Coke.

Suddenly a head appears outside the open drivers' side window startling RJ.

"Evening, old stain. Doing a little stargazing are we?"

"Jesus, Harry, you scared the shit out of me."

"I thought I smelled something, but I assumed it was that rather disgusting thing you're eating."

"What the fuck are you doing here, Harry?"

"You know, old stain, you have an extraordinary command of the King's English, truly remarkable."

"Cut the crap, Harry. What's going on?"

Harry climbs into the car and takes some of RJ's French fries.

"On my way home. I live not far from here and I happened to see your car. Who lives in the house?"

"House? What house?"

"That was a terrible line reading. It's a good thing you're not trying to make it as an actor. Nice field glasses."

Suddenly lights come on in the house and the pool area is fully illuminated followed by recorded music. Ginny and several other people come outside. A blond haired young man in his mid-twenties carries an ice bucket and two bottles of wine. He puts the wine and bucket on the bar and begins pouring. It is evident that the group is having a great time and has had plenty to drink. A guest lights a joint and passes it around. Harry now sits alongside RJ and has commandeered his binoculars.

"Happy little group. Anyone we know?"

"None of your goddamned business."

"Somehow I thought that might be your response. Consistent with your other two … or is it three … snappy retorts."

"My soon to be ex-wife, if you must know, the blond in the black dress."

"Handsome woman. How'd you ever let that one get away? I'll wager it's a long story."

"Harry … you know … sometimes … forget it."

"Consider it forgotten … whatever it was. Who's the young man?"

I think it might be her son. I haven't seen him in quite a while.

"Her son? Not the product of your alliance?"

"No. She was married once before me. When she was very young. Seventeen or eighteen I think. High school."

"Look a lot alike, don't they?"

"You think so? People used to say he looked like me.

I'm surprised he's here. They haven't gotten along in years. He lived with his grandfather, Ginny's father Dorsey, for a long time. Look Harry, I've had a long day. I'm tired and I need sleep. Would you mind getting out of the car?"

"Not a bit, dear boy. However, after all this intrigue I'm a bit parched. Would you fancy a nice cold beer? You wouldn't be a Guinness fan, per chance, would you?"

RJ, after a short consideration, "As a matter of fact I am. What have you got in mind?"

"A visit to the fat man. Not far. Shall we take your car? You can drop me back later."

"Fine."

Harry and RJ have arrived at Little Al's Bar and are nursing a couple of draught Guinness'. Little Al, an enormous man with a full beard and a shaved head, is tending bar.

"Her name is Ginny. It's really Virginia as in her name was Virginia. They called her Virgin for short, but not for long."

"What a terrible thing to grow up with. Did people actually say that to her?"

"All the time, started in high school. And I was not spying on her, by the way, in case you were wondering."

RJ looks at Harry as if seeing him for the first time.

"Tell me something, Harry. Just who are you?"

"I beg your pardon?"

"Who are you? Where are you from? What do you do?"

"As in for a living, I presume you mean."

"Exactly."

"Not much of anything, anymore. I made a bit some time ago. Managed to invest it rather well and I've been able to live comfortably ever since."

"How did you make the money initially?"

"I don't normally tell people this but I discovered, early on, that young men … many, many, young men as it turns out, were embarrassed about asking a pharmacist for a package of prophylactics. So, I went into the mail order business selling a variety of these particular items mailed in plain brown paper."

"Rubbers? You made your fortune selling rubbers through the mail?"

"Well, not a fortune … well, I suppose one could say a small fortune, yes."

"Harry MacDivitt the Rubber Baron. Amazing."

They sip their drinks each in his own rumination.

"So, what about this spying on your soon to be ex-wife business."

"I am not spying on my … on anybody. Didn't I just tell you that?"

"Sorry. But what would you call it then when you sit in a darkened automobile in the middle of the night watching her through a pair of binoculars?"

"My daughter also lives there. Wanted to see how she was doing. That's all."

"I see."

"Is that so strange?"

"Probably not, however, given the circumstances of your forthcoming divorce, whatever they are…."

"Not good."

Later that night RJ is having a hard time sleeping. He rolls and tosses. Finally turn on a light and checks the time: two-thirty three. He rolls over and is almost asleep when the phone rings.

"Hello. Hello!"

RJ slams the phone down.

"God dammit."

He tries to go back to sleep. No deal. He rolls over and turns on a small light and sits up. The phone rings again.

"Hello? Hello. God dammit!"

He starts to hang up.

"I hope I woke you. Are you alone?"

"Ginny?"

"Ah, you still recognize my voice. Must mean you haven't entirely forgotten me. Don't know how I feel about that."

"Jesus, Gin, what do you want? You know how I hate getting phone calls in the middle of the night. How'd you get my number?"

"Oh, I'm so sorry. Why don't you go back to sleep and I'll call you tomorrow and tell you what happened to Callie. Bye."

"Wait! Don't hang up. Ginny! Ginny?"

"Yeees."

"You're trying to drive me crazy aren't you?"

"Not a drive, in your case, just a short putt."

"Yeah, yeah, very funny. So what happened to Callie?"

"Nothing."

"Nothing? You called me at whatever the hell the time is to tell me nothing?"

"Oh, I'm sorry. She fell off her tricycle and broke her arm. Is that better?"

"Is that true? Did she really?"

"No."

"Ginny, what's going on?"

"I missed you and I just thought I'd call. So there. Strange, isn't it, the one thing I miss about you is sex. Who'd a thunk it?"

RJ doesn't know whether to believe this or not.

"Is this some kind of sick game? I'm going to hang up now."

"Wait. Where is Callie's birth certificate?"

"What? I don't know. Why do you need her birth certificate?"

"I want to enroll her in a swim class and I need to prove she's old enough."

"Old enough? They teach kids to swim when they're still in the womb. How old were you? Why do you need a birth certificate?"

"Nice trying to talk to you, RJ. Let me know if I can ever do something for you."

"Ginny? Ginny, don't hang up."

"Well…?"

"I'd like to see Callie tomorrow."

There is no answer from Ginny.

"Ginny? Are you there?"

"Yes. Fine. After lunch, Say, one o'clock."

She hangs up.

The next day RJ and Callie are sailing in a small day sailer and having a whale of a good time. Both are wearing life jackets. Callie also has a kid's captain's hat and sits on RJ's lap as he teaches her how to steer.

A slow day at the boat yard. No customers. RJ has a clipboard and is checking out a boat. He notices a car pull into the parking lot. A man gets out, sees RJ and heads toward him. It is Bob Greene from the Miami television station.

"Bob Greene, RJ. We met in Miami…"

"Yeah, Bob, how are you?"

"Fine, thanks."

"What brings you to Lauderdale? Interested in buying a boat."

"I wish. I came looking for you, actually."

"From the look on your face I assume this is not about a job offer."

"You assume correctly. I wish it was the case, however, it's not. I'm leaving the station. I'm on the way to L.A. Program Director. Kind of a lateral move, but a bigger market, as you know."

"Congratulations."

"Thanks. Look, something has been bothering me since we first met and I want to get it off my chest."

"When you came to see me about the job I told you the position had already been filled. That wasn't true. In fact they're still looking for someone."

"I'm not...."

"That isn't it. Let me finish. My boss had a few too many at my going away party. Same thing has been bothering him. He told me the story. It seems you've got an enemy who knows a lot of people. Calls were made. He doesn't know who's after your ass, but it's someone with a lot of clout."

Weeks fly by. RJ is enjoying the new job and has even made a couple of sales. Nothing big, but a good start. Frankie King seems pleased and he and RJ are beginning a very nice friendship.

RJ's bedroom very early in the morning. RJ is just waking up when the phone rings.

"Jesus, Ginny...."

"RJ, it's Mother. I have some terrible news. Ginny's mother just called me. Callie is dead. She drowned in the swimming pool."

"Nooo!"

"I'm on my way to the airport I'll meet you at the funeral home. Got a pencil?"

RJ and his mother are met in the hallway of the funeral home by the Funeral Director and are escorted to a visitation room that contains a few chairs, some flowers and a small casket. The room is devoid of people. RJ looks awful. Unshaven, eyes are puffy and he looks very shaky.

The Funeral Director, says, "I've arranged with the other side of the family for you and your mother to spend some time alone with your daughter."

"Thank you."

RJ and Lilly approach the casket.

RJ has been able to keep it all together up until this point. But he is about to lose it entirely when the door to the room opens and Ginny enters with her mother, her stepfather Robert, and Dorsey. Ginny seems in control until she sees RJ. Then, inexplicably, she becomes hysterical.

"I want my baby back. I want my baby!"

Her mother Helena admonishes her, "Now, Virginia, we'll have no histrionics."

RJ says, "Would you leave us alone for a few minutes? Everyone. Please."

Lilly is a bit perturbed, as is Helene. Neither likes the idea of being asked to leave, especially in the company of the other. They all do, however, depart, leaving RJ and Ginny alone. They just look at each other for the longest time, neither knowing what to say.

The door opens and the Director enters.

I'm sorry to bother you, Mr. Tyler, but there's a woman here who wants to see you. She says she was your daughter's baby sitter.

"Oh, god,"

"She says she has to leave soon."

Ginny doesn't like this idea at all.

"Would you, please, ask her to wait?"

"Of course."

"Thank you."

As the Director leaves Ginny's hysteria returns.

"Don't listen to her. She's a mean, vengeful, horrible person. She … she lies and she steals. I had to fire her."

"Hold it, hold it! Jesus, Gin…"

An interim while Ginny tries to regain control of herself.

"What difference does it make…"

"You don't know her. She's a gypsy … a witch. She…"

"Oh, come on."

Another pause while they both try to settle down.

"I want a cigarette."

She starts fumbling through her purse.

"You're going to smoke in here?"

"Why not? Who's going to complain? Callie? Huh? You want one?"

"No, thank you."

She lights up.

"So, how did it happen?"

"She fell into the swimming pool and drowned."

She starts looking around the room for an ashtray, and, of course, there isn't one.

"There's got to be more to it than that. I thought she was taking swimming lessons."

"She was to start today."

"Who was watching her? Didn't the alarm go off?"

"No alarm. There isn't one."

"A small child in the house and no alarm in the pool?"

"That's right."

Not finding an ashtray she flicks her ashes on the floor and grinds them into the carpeting.

"Why, why wasn't…."

"Look! No alarm. Got it. I didn't get around to putting one in. End of story."

RJ is having a very hard time with this. He hates asking these questions, but feels he must.

"Where were you when it happened?"

"In the kitchen with that stupid woman."

(Indicating the maid in the outer room).

She has come to the end of her smoke. She lights another one from the butt end and puts out the old one in a plant stand.

She starts to cry.

"Why didn't you call me?"

"I was too … distraught. Is that the word?"

"I don't know. Is it?"

"You're so … so … fucking proper. Such a good little boy. Even in bed. You make me sick."

Stung. RJ remains silent.

"I'm sorry. I didn't mean that. I know it's my fault. What can I do?"

"Do? About what? You can't do anything. There's nothing to do. She's gone."

"And it's all my fault, right? How about taking a little of the blame yourself mister perfect husband and father. Has it occurred to you that if you had worked a little harder on our marriage that this might not have happened? Goddammit!"

Ginny starts to cry. RJ, unable to keep his anguish intact, moves to Ginny and takes her in his arms and comforts her. Ginny cries even harder. In her misery she forgets the lit cigarette and almost sets RJ on fire, burning him slightly on the neck.

"Ow! Jesus, Ginny…"

"Sorry. Sorry."

She takes one more huge drag off the smoke and puts it into the pot with the other one.

"Maybe it's time for me to quit, too."

"Before you kill someone."

"That's really it, isn't it? You think I killed her, don't you?"

"I didn't say that."

"You don't have to, you smug bastard."

"Hey!"

In the heat of the moment Ginny has managed to misplace her purse.

"Where the fuck's my purse?"

She finds it and heads for the door.

RJ looks in the coffin one more time and emits an enormous, anguished, sob.

In the funeral home lobby Lilly is seated on a sofa by herself. She looks very pale. RJ enters wiping his eyes with a handkerchief.

"Mother? Are you all right?"

"I just had a conversation with a Mrs. Garcia. She was Callie's sitter. I think you should talk to her."

"Where is she?"

"She left. She seems frightened. She didn't want to see Ginny. I think she's afraid of her."

"What did she say?"

"She said one of Ginny's boy friends had thrown Raggedy Anne into the swimming pool shortly before Callie drowned. Evidently there'd been a lot of drinking. Maybe some drugs."

"God…"

"What do you make of it?"

"I don't know. Negligence at the very least, I suspect."

The next day RJ is seated in the lobby of the Fort Lauderdale Police Department. A large bald headed man in his late fifties approaches him.

"Mr. Tyler?"

RJ stands. "Yes?"

"I'm Lieutenant Beck. Will you come with me please?"

RJ follows Beck into an interior office. Beck sits behind the desk and motions for RJ to sit on the opposite side.

"What can I do for you?"

"I'm not sure if you can do anything. Some advice, perhaps. My daughter died last week and…"

"I know about the drowning. I'm very sorry. It must be very difficult for you."

"Yes, thank you. I still can't believe it."

Beck is very patient, letting RJ proceed at his own pace.

"The reason I'm here … there was a woman … baby sitter…house sitter … who was at the house the day my daughter died. Evidently she saw some things … a lot of drinking … drugs maybe … she talked to my mother at the funeral home … Callie's favorite doll…Raggedy Ann …being thrown into the swimming pool…."

"Mr. Tyler, before you go on, where is this woman now?"

"Well, that's the thing. I don't know. The only way I can find her is to talk to my ex-wife and I don't think that's such a good idea. Particularly now."

"And you'd like us to talk to your ex-wife and find out about the maid…."

"Right. I guess so. Can you do that?"

"Of course, if we suspect a crime has been committed."

Beck opens a drawer in the desk.

"If you'll just fill out this form. Your ex-wife's name, address, phone number. How we can get in touch with you. We'll look into it."

RJ and Lilly are at the airport waiting for her plane.

"I'm sorry, RJ. I wish I could stay longer. I must get back. You know how your father gets when I'm gone."

"Yeah, hungry."

"That mouth of yours. I swear it's going to get you in trouble someday."

"Already has. Several times. Some guys never learn."

"I talked to the police this morning."

"What did they say?"

"They're going to check it out. Talk to the baby sitter."

"I think the flight is boarding. Take care of yourself, Mother. Thanks for coming down. I couldn't have made it without you."

"You don't give yourself credit. You're a lot stronger than you think you are. In a strange way it might be for the best. Who knows how she would have turned out with that woman for a mother."

"Mother, for God's sake…. I think you'd better get on the plane."

They hug. Lilly boards and RJ bolts for the entrance in a rage.

RJ is driving way too fast …swerving in and out of traffic. He manages to see a cop car moving in the other direction and this causes him to slow down a bit. At the next exit he pulls off. He parks his car in the lot of a municipal park and runs as fast as he can through the open field. When he can run no further he stops, catches his breath, and screams into the night.

"Why!!!"

RJ and Harry are having a drink on the veranda of Harry's house that overlooks the pool. It's the first time RJ has been here and he is favorably impressed.

"This place is pretty terrific. Must have cost a bloody fortune."

"Wasn't a bargain, that's for sure. You don't look too bad all things considered."

"Looks can be deceiving they tell me. If truth be told I'm a god awful mess and I don't seem to be getting any better."

Harry picks up a pack of cigarettes and offers one to RJ.

"No thanks."

"Did you ever smoke?"

"Oh, yeah. Big time. I can even remember the first time I tried it. I must have been about six or seven…maybe eight. My maternal grandparents had a small farm on the edge of town. Close enough that my pals Gary and Ronnie and I could walk there. Both my grandparents, Gladys and Fred smoked. Camels for him. Marvel's for her. I stole a pack …I think it was the Marvel's and my little pals and I ran up the hill behind the farmhouse to what they called the "back forty." There was a pretty good-sized fallen tree trunk that had been lying there for some time. We climbed up and took out a cigarette. Since I was the thief I got to take the first puff which I did the same way I'd seen the way my grandfather do it. One huge inhale. Knocked me right off the back of the log. I wasn't knocked out, but damn close. "Wow, so that's what smoking is!" Should have quit right then and there."

RJ and Harry both laugh at this and then a pall settles over the veranda.

Finally Harry says, "I wonder what's worse: losing a child when it is very young or when it's much older. "An adult say."

RJ considers this for a few moments than says, "I think it's worse when they're young; you don't have many memories. You wonder what they might have been. How they would have turned out. At least when they're older…" And then he lets out a huge agonizing sob.

"Oh, God… why…why…why."

"I don't know. I just can't tell you how sorry I am. It all seems so pointless."

"It didn't have to end this way. We should have been able to work things out. I feel so guilty. Like it's my fault she died and I couldn't save her."

"Don't beat yourself up, RJ. It's not your fault."

"You know what's weird. Since Callie died I can't whistle. What's that mean?"

"I have no idea."

"Ginny didn't want to have another child. Chase was a young adult when Callie was born. Living with Ginny's father… still does… for reasons I'm not privy to. Ginny used to say that in the case of Callie it only took one to tango. She said that I had willed it to happen. She may have been right. No doubt about it, I wanted that baby."

"Refill?"

"Please. I just don't understand. Somewhere along the line I became the enemy. And I had to be punished. She and that father of hers '…."

"What's he like, the father?"

"It's hard to say. It's like he's adrift, anchorless."
"Kinda' like you, Harry."

"Careful."

57

"Big difference you're not evil. You not evil are you Harry?"

"Only around the edges."

"I don't think I want to know what that means. He inherited a ton of money when he was in college during the Depression and he literally hasn't worked a day in his life. He got himself a commission in the navy. During the war he was stationed in Havana and Miami. He told Ginny the hardest part of his job was getting enough dress uniforms for the cocktail parties. He and Ginny's mother were only married for a couple of years. Now she can't stand him. He never remarried. He's been everywhere, done everything. So, now all he does is interfere with other people's lives. Like Ginny's. And mine."

"And she adores him?"

"Yeah, maybe now, but not always. There was a time when they didn't speak for over three years. I talked her into calling him shortly after Callie was born. Big, teary reconciliation over the phone. A couple of weeks later he came to visit. Loaded with presents. Before he got there Ginny was a wreck. Never without a cigarette in her hand. She'd start to drink mid-afternoon. I should have listened more carefully to her. Seen what kind of a man he was. The hold he had on his daughter."

"I can't prove it, but I know he got me fired from C.B.S. and I suspect he had a hand in my not getting the Miami job as well."

"Why would he do that?"

"I don't have a clue. Up till we were getting divorced I'd only met him that one time. Thought he liked me."

"How'd he do that... getting you fired?"

"I don't know, the old boy network, maybe. Why is it, Harry, that all the bad guys wind up in first place?"

"I don't know. I have no idea."

"They're not going to get away with this. I'll get even with them if it takes … if it takes…"

RJ breaks into tears. Harry hands him another drink.

"Thanks."

RJ is moving into his new apartment. He is getting another load out of his car as Harry pulls up in a new bright red Corvette convertible; hair cut, face shaved and instead of the dirty chinos and the faded Hawaiian sport shirt, he is decked out in a new sport coat, tailored slacks and colorful, but tasteful, open-necked shirt. He seems wary about parking in this neighborhood.

"Nice car."

"Yes, thank you."

Harry is still concerned with his car being boosted.

"You don't look so good."

"Wonder why? You're dangerous, Harry. If I didn't know better I'd think you were trying to get me drunk last night."

"Nobody twisted your arm."

"Yeah, right. Never again, he lied. You on the other hand look very … smart."

"Whatever that means."

Harry is perusing the neighborhood.

"How're you doin'?"

"Fine. Fine."

An enormous, and seemingly vicious, black dog that is tied to a tree in the yard next door starts barking at Harry. Harry takes a suitcase and as the boys head for the front door he takes one more concerned look at his new car. RJ gives Harry the fifty-cent tour. Harry is less than favorably impressed. He looks as if he smells a dead rat.

"You can't be serious. You're actually going to live here?"

"Come on, Harry, it's not that bad."

"No, it's worse. Have you taken a close look at your neighbors? It looks like a casting call for a prison movie out there."

"Harry…"

They have walked through the bedroom and are now in the bathroom. Harry lifts the lid, peers into the toilet.

"Gawd!"

RJ and Lt. Beck are walking along the pier. They stop at a seventy-foot sailboat.

"Oh, that's a beauty. How much is that one?"

"Big bucks. Practically brand new. Shall I write it up?"

"Yeah, right. On a cop's salary."

"So, what's the story? Any news?"

"Not really. I talked to your ex. Ask her about the doll being thrown in the swimming pool … drugs. Nothin'. Didn't know what I was talkin' about."

"Figures. What about the sitter?"

"San Salvador. I talked to her neighbors. She and her family came into some money and moved back home. Left very quickly. Looks like a dead end. We gave it a shot. That's about all we can do."

"Well, it was worth a try. Not going to bring my daughter back anyway. Wait a minute. You think Ginny paid her off to get her out of the country so that she couldn't testify?"

"Anything is possible. But there's nothing we can do about it based on hearsay. We gave it a shot. Well, I'd better be going."

Beck heads off down the pier back to his car.

"Wait a minute! This bitch is stoned out of her tits … fucking her brains out … while my daughter is drowning

… and all you can say is "We gave it a shot?" Well, it's not enough. Not by a long shot."

Beck is stunned by this outburst, as are other people in the boat yard.

RJ's room at the Ocean Ranch. The sliding glass doors to the balcony are open and a gentle breeze blows the curtains. RJ and Ginny are in bed together.

"We probably shouldn't be doing this."

"But, we are. The question is … why?"

"Because, we're going to make another Callie."

"What? That's … that's."

"That's … what?"

"I don't know."

RJ is suddenly very nervous. Something is wrong here.

"Come on, RJ you can do it. Stick it in me. Let's make a baby."

"No, no. I … I can't."

"How silly of me. Of course you can't. You can't make it now and you couldn't make it then. And that's why you're not Callie's father."

"What? What are you talking about?"

"Here's your baby, RJ. Here's the only child you ever had." Ginny reaches under the bed and starts hitting RJ with Raggedy Ann. RJ awakes screaming. He is standing trapped in a corner of his new bedroom room with the wind blown drapes wrapped around his head.

The boys are seated at a table outside a dockside restaurant. RJ is looking at a menu while Harry rather intently watches two men tie up a sailboat.

"So, how are you bearing up?"

"I'm okay. Sorta'."

"Must be tough."

"I hope you never know."

Harry returns his attention to the boaters. RJ checks out Harry.

"I swear, Harry, when you drove up the other day in your new car I almost didn't recognize you."

"Well, to be perfectly frank, I thought it about time I changed the way I strut my stuff … as it were."

"Why?"

"I was invited, Monday, I believe it was, to have lunch with an old friend at the Pompano Beach Country Club. My previous incarnation didn't seem terribly appropriate to the occasion."

"In other words you were afraid they wouldn't let you in."

"Something along those lines, yes."

Harry returns his gaze to the boaters.

"So how was the lunch?"

"Hum?"

"With the old friend."

"Ah. Interesting. Not so much with the company as with the surroundings … very old money, as it were. Your ex is a member. You are officially divorced aren't you?"

"Almost. How do you know she's a member?"

"Saw her there, with her son. Brilliantly handsome lad. He works there. Teaches golf. The ladies love him, as you can well imagine."

A waiter approaches.

"A drink, gentleman?"

"Yeah. Harry, what are you having?"

"Bacardi light rum and club soda with a squeeze of lime."

"Make it two."

"You look like you're getting a tan."

Harry, feeling his face, "Well, I suppose I am, actually. Been spending a lot of time outside. Practicing."

"Practicing? Practicing what? Golf?"

"Yes, indeed. Golf. I've been taking lessons. Ginny tells me I should wear a hat and sun block, but it seems…"

"Hang on there a minute, Mr. Hogan. "Ginny tells me?""

"We've met. Didn't I mention that?"

"You told me you had lunch with your friend. You didn't say anything about meeting Ginny."

"Are you sure?"

"Harry…"

"Well, anyway, I'm taking lessons."

"From Chase?"

"He's very good. I should be on the Tour any day now."

"Wait. Stop. You and Ginny meet. You drooled and she said wear a hat? What else?"

"Nothing much, really. We've had lunch once or twice."

"Lunch! What the hell is going on here? Lunch?"

"Why not? I thought I might be useful. Be a help in whatever it is you're planning."

"Planning? I'm not planning anything."

The waiter brings the drinks.

""I'll get her if it's the last thing I ever do". Or words to that effect."

"I said that? I don't remember…"

"Not once, but several times. Emphatically."

"Well, if I did it was just the booze talking. I didn't mean…"

"Oh, I think you did. Most assuredly."

"All right, let's say you're right. So what? What are you getting at?"

"I think there is a lot to your story that you neglected to tell me. Your being homosexual for instance and…"

"What!"

"And a convicted child abuser."

"What the hell are you talking about?"

"Not to mention the times you beat that poor woman to within an inch of her life."

RJ is incredulous.

"You can deny it all you wish, but those are some of the stories Ginny has been telling to her cronies at the club."

"I don't know what to say. Why is she doing this?"

"I don't know. I try to give her a sympathetic ear. She doesn't know me from Adam, of course. At least she doesn't know I know you. You might find that useful."

"The spy who came in from the driving range?"

"In a manner of speaking. Jesus, I'd like a smoke."

"You quit?"

"Yes, a week or so ago."

"Congratulations. Now that you mention it I don't believe I've noticed you coughing."

"They sit in silence for a moment. RJ is still in shock thinking about Harry's recent tale about Ginny."

"On to a lighter subject. Your current abode. Though not all that lighter if you consider the lack of windows and the…"

"Come on, Harry, my apartment's not that bad."

"Yes, it definitely is. After we've had lunch, I want you to hop into your cute little car and follow me. I want to show you something that I think you will find immensely interesting."

RJ and Harry pull into the underground parking garage of a very attractive condominium building in their respective cars, enter the elevator, and ride to the fourth floor. The top floor as it turns out. Harry has the keys and they enter the apartment.

RJ can only say, "Wow! Who lives here?"

The living room contains a big screen television set, matching Eames lounge chairs and ottomans, a state of the art stereo system, glass dining table with leather and chrome chairs, etc.

"It belongs to a friend of mine. He'd like to sell it, but thinks there's a glut of condos on the market right now, and if he tries to dump it, he's going to lose a bundle. So, he's willing to rent it."

"How much?"

"Dirt cheap. He owes me a couple of favors."

"How old is this guy?"

"What a strange question? Why do you ask?"

"The way it's decorated. He must be very young. No Leroy Neiman? Round or water bed?"

RJ heads into the bedroom. Harry goes into the kitchen where he takes a couple of beers out of the fridge and pours them into frosted pewter mugs.

"Nope. Your basic king."

"Let's take a look at the balcony."

The boys walk out onto the balcony. RJ looks across the Intracoastal Waterway towards Ginny's house.

RJ is not aware of Harry.

"RJ ... RJ, are you all right?"

"Yeah, fine."

"You didn't recognize it when we drove up?"

"Looks different in the daytime. I've only seen it from ground level."

The parking lot across the waterway.

"Right."

"It really is a lovely house. Expensive."

"She can afford it. Her grandfather set her up in some kind of trust fund and then there's her father... Mr. Money Bags."

"And it all goes to Chase eventually?"

"The whole deal. Now that there's no one else."

"Interesting. You could throw a baseball into that pool from here."

"Or a hand grenade. I don't know, Harry, it's a nice place, but, I'd hate to walk out on the balcony some morning and see her looking at me through a telescope, you know what I mean?"

"Absolutely. Well, it was just a thought."

RJ looks over the balcony again towards Ginny's house just as she comes outside in a bikini.

"So, when can I move in?"

RJ is browsing in the bedding department of a local department store. In his cart he has pillows, packages of pillowcases, bath towels and various other items for his new apartment. Suddenly, seemingly out of nowhere, comes the cry of a banshee.

"What the fuck are you doing?"

RJ turns to see Ginny, hands on hips, looking like several million bucks, glaring at him. She is with Dorsey and a woman about Ginny's age, also a looker, but no match for the Gin. The friend has no idea what is going on or who this man is.

"Hey, asshole, are you following me? Suzy, if this prick tries to talk to you kick him in the balls and call a cop. We have laws about people like you. And speaking of cops ... what's with sticking that guy ... what's his name ... Beck? ... on me?"

RJ can't seem to find his tongue. He tries to put back the plastic wrapped sheets he has been looking at and in the process knocks over the entire pile. He attempts, in vain, to catch them, exacerbating the problem.

"Hey! I'm talking to you. Yoo hoo. Anybody home?"

"I ... I..."

"Ay, yi, yi, South America take it away. Carmen Miranda. Lousy impersonation. Then again the only thing you could imitate is a falling down drunk. Come on, Daddy let's go, something stinks in here. I think you ought to try the pink number with the spider lace around the bottom. Matches your eyes."

As RJ watches them exit the area another stack of sheets falls to the floor. RJ picks them up as Ginny returns, alone this time. They stare at each other for a moment.

"Something on your mind?"

She's gone, RJ. Give it up. Get on with your life.

"What are you talking about?"

"Look at yourself. You never were a whole lot. Now you're a mess. And you're making me nervous being here. Why don't you leave? Go back to Chicago where you belong."

"Boy, you don't lack for balls do you? You don't run my life. You did at one time, but not anymore."

"Maybe. Maybe not. We'll see."

"Whatever that means."

Ginny walks up to RJ and using both hands, pushes him into a pile of towels knocking him over.

"You're pathetic, you fucking wimp. You really are."

RJ walks across the nearly deserted department store parking lot toward his car. His arms are loaded with four large shopping bags. He is only faintly aware of a car coming up alongside him. Suddenly the car accelerates and the driver reaches out and hits RJ in the back of the neck sending him ass over applecart, the contents of the bags flying in all directions. RJ gets up gingerly, limping as the white car exits the lot.

Late one Sunday RJ is having a sandwich and a beer and scanning Ginny's pool area with his binoculars. He has an ice pack on his knee. The phone rings.

"Hello? Oh, hi, Frankie."

"My secretary told me about your accident. How're ya' doin'?"

"I'm okay. A little sore. No broken bones."

"You want to take a couple of days off?"

"No, I'm fine."

"Whatever you say. She also told me about your new place. Sounds great. You'll have to have me over for dinner. I'll bring a friend or two."

"Great."

"Listen compadre, I'm thinking of taking an old forty or fifty foot sloop on consignment and I want you to take a look at her. Belongs to a friend of mine. Older guy. Recently lost his wife. You know about wooden hulls?"

"Yeah, they break easily and they leak."

"Not always. Anyway, get your ass down to Coconut Grove and look up a guy by the name of Arbuthnot. He's staying at the Grand Bay Hotel. He's expecting to hear from you."

"What's his name?"

"Ar-buth-not. Spelled just like it sounds. First name's Ray. Boat's called the Baracuta with a 't'. Check it out. Got another call. Gotta' go."

RJ walks out of the Grand Bay Hotel with a piece of paper in his hand detailing the directions to the boat. As he walks to the marina he sees a large banner on the side of the Miami Convention Center announcing the GREATER MIAMI KNIFE AND GUN SHOW AND SALE. HALF PRICE TICKETS ON WEDNESDAY AND THURSDAY.

As he approaches the row of moored boats that the map indicates is the location of the sailboat a sixtyish man wearing a captain's hat is waving a flag showing a naked woman holding a Martini glass at RJ. He is standing in the stern of the Baracuta next to a FOR SALE sign. RJ is momentarily stopped in his tracks. He can't believe his eyes.

"You RJ McCaw?"

"Yes. You must be Mr. Ar…"

"Ray, please. Call me Ray. Come on board."

"Nice flag."

"I got tons of 'um. From all over the world. Runnin' out of places to store 'um. Drives my wife … oh, shit."

"I was sorry to hear about your wife. Frankie told me."

"I still can't believe she's gone. Make yourself at home. Look around. She's a beauty, isn't she?"

"Gorgeous."

They move toward the bow. RJ examines the rigging and looks below as they walk.

"I'll tell you, Mr. Ar … Ar…"

"Ray."

"Right. Ray. I know this boat well. I have a friend who has one on Lake Michigan. Belmont Harbor. I've sailed it for years. If I could afford it I'd buy it myself. But, you know…"

"Yeah, I know wooden hulls."

"Not necessarily a bad thing. I was thinking about what I could afford and, as they say, this ain't it."

"I think it would be a good idea if we had a nautical engineer check it out. Wouldn't want to get someone interested in buying it then discovering a problem."

"Right. Good idea. Can you set it up?"

"Of course. Happy to. It would probably be better if we could get it to our boat yard."

"No problem. I'll take care of it."

RJ heads back in the direction of his parked car. He once again notices the Knife and Gun Show banner which also reads: DON'T BUY A GUN … UNTIL YOU'VE SEEN ALL THE NEAT STUFF AT THE SHOW THAT IS. Hungry RJ decides to have lunch before he heads back home. He's seated at the outdoor bar of a restaurant that is on the second floor of the COCO WALK shopping and restaurant complex. A waiter sets a drink in front of him. RJ takes a sip of the drink and picks up a throw away newspaper that someone has left on the bar. A woman's laugh draws his attention to the street below. Ginny has Chase and Harry in tow. They are laughing at something Harry is saying and all three seem to be having one hell of a good time. They eventually come to a restaurant with outdoor tables where they join Dorsey. RJ watches them for a while and then says out loud to himself, "Well, well, well. What a happy little group. I wonder what you're all up to."

A short time later as RJ is walking back to his car he has a change of mind and decides to take a look at the gun show.

To say RJ was unfamiliar with firearms would be a gross understatement. His father had a twenty-two caliber pistol which he never fired and kept locked in a drawer. His grandfather had a 410 shotgun that he said was for varmints.

RJ had heard a lot about guns; Smith and Wesson, Browning, Colt, but they were just names to him. When

70

he walked around the enormous display at the gun show he was almost overwhelmed with the variety of firearms and not just guns but whips, knives, hand cuffs. You name it, it was there and much more. Books on every imaginable topic from riot control to how to disappear; as in leaving the country. One title that caught his eye was how to be your own dick. Was this about how to become a detective or some kind of self-help from California? He didn't have the courage to pick it up to find out...even in a hall full of strangers.

Many of the display tables were so crowded with potential customers that it was difficult to get close enough to see what they were actually selling.

RJ found himself thinking seriously about buying a gun. You get caught up in the fever at these shows he was beginning to realize and before long you begin to believe that, yes, I really do need a gun or two or three.

But what kind of a gun? A shotgun? Splatter her all over Pompano Beach.

A pistol? What was the difference between a pistol and a revolver? He had no idea and was too embarrassed to ask someone.

In fact he knew exactly what he wanted and had known from the first moment he stepped out onto his balcony and looked across at Ginny's house: a rifle with a telescopic site.

RJ returned to a display table he had passed earlier and a rifle that had caught his eye. Mostly handguns on this table with some shotguns and...there it was. REMINGTON 30-06 WITH CUSTOM STOCK AND TRIPOD. MATT BLACK FINISH WITH NO SHINY SURFACES TO CATCH THE LIGHT AND ALERT THE VICTIM.

RJ imagined himself wearing all black with a balaclava covering his head and just to be on the safe side his face covered with black makeup or whatever it was commandos wore in all those World War Two movies. Four hundred and ninety five dollars.

RJ is unaware of a man having walked up behind him.

"A steal."

"You think so?"

"Absolutely."

"Must be noisy."

"Oh, yeah. Hell of a bang."

RJ thinks to himself that what he does not need is to call attention to where the shot or shots came from and he starts to walk on.

"Wait a sec. You serious about buying a firearm?"

"Yeah, I guess you could say I'm serious, but I need something that would be accurate, with practice of course, from say a hundred and fifty to two hundred yards and at night. Oh, and relatively quiet."

"You're not a farmer are you? You don't look like a farmer. Not that there's anything wrong about looking like a farmer."

RJ laughs, "No I am definitely not a farmer."

"A cop?"

"I sell boats."

A gun at the end of the table that is barely covered with a black cloth catches his eye.

"What's that one?"

"You don't see many of those at your run of the mill gun shows."

"It looks military. Is the, ah…"

"Stock."

"Right. Stock wooden? Doesn't look like it."

"Fiberglass. Extremely light weight for so powerful a gun. Comes in a walnut stock in the target models. This one's a sniper rifle. Three-oh-eight Winchester. Ten shot magazine. And as you can see this one has a telescopic and as you can see the whole outfit is camouflaged."

"How much is it?"

"This here is a used gun. Not used much, but I can't sell it as new. I sold it to the original owner. He was going to join one of them Para-military outfits that are going to save us from whatever it is that is threatening us at the moment. This guy was a little too squirrely even for those guys. Told him to take a hike. Can you imagine what kind of a wacko you have to be to get turned down by those guys? So I bought the gun back from him."

"Well, at least he doesn't have the gun anymore."

"No, not this one anyways."

"So, what do you want for it?"

"What does the tag say? Can't read it without my glasses."

"Nine hundred and fifty dollars. Wow! Lotta' money. Does that include the scope and the tripod?"

"Bipod. Only has two legs. Like a man."

"Oh, yeah, right. Bipod. Learn something every day."

"You do if you keep your eyes open."

It is evident that RJ really wants this gun.

"I'll tell you what I'll do. I've had this piece for quite some time and frankly I'd like to sell it. Not much of a market for this kinda' weapon these days. Everybody seems to want some hi-tech semi-automatic something or other. Well, anyway I do ramble on. Look, I'm about to retire. Not takin' any new inventory. I'll tell you what I'll do. If you take it right now, today, so that I don't have to cart it back to the shop I'll give it to you, including the bipod and the scope for eight-fifty…make that eight hundred even and I'll throw in a box of cartridges. What do you say?"

"You take a check?"

A week later a crane is lowering the Baracuta into the water at Frankie's boat yard as RJ and Frankie watch.

"Well, Frankie, what do you think?"

"I think we're going to be lookin' at this one for a long, long, time."

The parking lot at Little Al's bar. RJ and Harry arrive in their respective cars simultaneously. Harry in his modus vivendi: expensive chino slacks, silk polo shirt, brown and white saddle shoes, alpaca sweater over the shoulders. RJ, on the other hand is wearing ... RJ stuff. They shake hands and walk toward the entrance.

"Hey, Harry, how ya' doin? Nice trip?"

"Trip?"

"The Grove. I saw you there over the weekend, with Ginny and Chase and the old man. Looked like you were having a good time, a real good time."

Harry stops walking and grabs RJ's arm.

"Wait a minute. That sounds almost like an accusation."

"Wear it any way it fits. You're supposed to be helping me and I'm beginning to get the distinct impression that you're planning on moving in with her instead. What are you now, about a six handicap?"

"Not quite, but I did break a hundred this week for the first time."

"Harry, I can't tell you how happy that makes me."

RJ says to an imaginary person: "Garçon, a bottle of your best bubbly for my semi-close personal friend Harry the hundred breaker."

"Why are you so riled up? What have I done to deserve this diatribe?"

RJ, suddenly contrite, replies, "Nothing. Nothing. Just forget it."

"No, I'm not going to forget it. All I...."

"All right, all right. Hold it down. I'm just getting very frustrated with all this dickin' around. I got word this morning I'm officially divorced. And today is our anniversary. How's that for coincidence?"

"Congratulations."

"Go fuck yourself, Harry, and the Corvette you came in on."

Harry choses to ignore this.

"I bought a gun. No more screwing around. Pop her once and that's it. And maybe her old man in the process. The sooner the better."

RJ turns and heads back to his car.

"RJ, wait a second."

"I'll see you later, Harry. Maybe."

Harry is at a loss as to what to do. He stops to think, giving RJ just enough time to get in his car and drive off.

Early one misty Sunday morning RJ is driving in the Everglades along a highway known as Alligator Alley. He appears to be looking for something. He drives past the Seminole Indian reservation. He finally sees what he is looking for and pulls off onto a dirt road leading into a glade. No houses. No gas stations. No buildings. Desolate. After a few minutes he stops and gets out of the car. He takes the rifle, a handful of bullets, and a box of empty bottles and cans. He paces off what he imagines is an equivalent distance between his balcony and Ginny's pool area. He hangs a large coke bottle from a low hanging tree limb, loads, sights, and fires. Doesn't hit a thing. The sound is fairly loud, but not enough to hurt his ears. He can deal with it.

He puts another round in the chamber and fires again. Still no success. He takes out a Swiss Army knife, adjusts the rifle's rear sight, and tries again. The bottle breaks into a thousand pieces.

Bingo.

RJ hangs another bottle. He chambers a round, but before he can shoulder the rifle the bottle shatters and a split second later he hears the shot. RJ quickly turns around and scans the horizon, but can't see anything clearly because he is looking directly into the sun which has just come out through the mist. Another shot, this time very close to RJ who dives for cover. In the distance what appears to be a large white car pulls away in a cloud of dust.

The next morning was a toughie. RJ, although he hated to admit it to himself, he was still shaken by being shot at. Although he'd gone through a lot of trauma in his life this was a first and he didn't like it at all.

"Jesus Christ, you look like shit."

"Thank you, Frank. And top of the mornin' to you, too."

"You had any coffee?"

"I don't think it will help. Especially that stuff your secretary calls coffee."

"What's with you? You got the rag on?"

"Sorry. Little out of sorts. Might be getting a cold."

"Okay. No big deal. You'll never guess what happened last night?"

"You had a little strange? Your wife?"

"Very funny, but not even close. I sold a boat to André de Benedetti."

"You're kidding. Who's…what's his name?"

"Big time lawyer. Very low key. Nobody even knows where for sure he lives. Might be the Everglades somewhere. Who knows? Rumor has it he's loaded. He got my number somehow and called me at eleven

76

o'clock at home. 'Just happened to be driving by the boat yard and saw that bright red Cigarette Boat. Tell me about it.' So I gave him all the details: what size engine, how many hours it's got on it, the price. All that shit. He listens for no more than two or three minutes and says 'I'll take it. My guy'll come tomorrow morning to pay for it. Will a check be all right?' At nine o'clock sharp in walks this Cuban guy in a silk suit. Says his name is Felipe Lobo. I think that means wolf. Anyway, he says he represents Mr. de Benedetti and he hands me a check for the entire amount. Drives off in the boat."

"How'd he get to the yard?"

"Took a cab, or got a ride, or walked. How the fuck should I know? The important thing is de Benedetti actually bought the friggin' boat. Two hundred and fifty thousand dollars worth of ninety mile an hour power."

"Amazing. And a hell of a price."

"Wonder what he's gonna' do with a cigarette boat in the glades?"

"Take his mother to church. Sometimes you ask the most dumb assed questions. You can ask him when you get down there."

"Down there? Down where?"

"He has to sign the paper work. You're expendable for a day."

"You let him have the boat with a check and without signing a contract?"

"A guy writes you a check for a quarter of a million dollars. You going to turn him down because he's not there to sign the paperwork? Besides, this guy's face is more familiar in this part of the world than the fucking Governor's!"

"Yeah, but still…"

"Schmuck. Is this your money? Stop worryin' about it. Drop by the office and get the file. Get a hundred bucks in expense money. Hop in your little car and get your ass down to the Keys. The errand boy's going to meet you at a place called Sweaty's in Marathon around noon. He'll take you to André's place. I think he lives in the Bay somewhere."

"In the bay? What's that mean 'in the bay someplace'? What bay?"

"The booze startin' to eat your fuckin' brain? Florida Bay, like I told you before. Rumor has it his place is a cross between a key and a glade. Used to be some kinda' military base during the war. Who knows? What am I a fuckin' tour guide? Just get the stuff signed and don't worry about it."

RJ says, "Look, I'm no expert on Florida and I've never been to the keys, but I read in the paper a few months ago that there were no inhabited islands in the bay other than the ones that were connected by Highway One on the way to Key West. Also, according to this article, there haven't been any private homes in the Everglades since a big hurricane came through in the late forties. So where the hell is this place anyway?"

"Nowhere."

"Nowhere?"

"That's right. As far as you're concerned it's fucking nowhere. It doesn't exist."

"Must make getting mail difficult. What's the zip code for nowhere?"

Sweaty's faced the Bahamas. The bar wasn't air-conditioned. Open air. Overhead fans. And then there was Sweaty. What a guy. All three hundred odd pounds of him. Tons of fun. This citizen and Little Jack could be the world's largest book ends.

The old sweat-master is plagued by some kind of condition whereby he perspires all the time. Regardless of the temperature. Exceedingly sudoriparous: producing or secreting sweat. He'd looked it up once. A real problem in Pittsburgh, where he came from (Pirates memorabilia all over the bar), but hardly noticeable in south Florida where being perpetually damp is a way of life. Still, a good guy to stay upwind of on a hot day.

He'd been there about half an hour when the Cigarette Boat pulled up to the pier and the scariest man he'd ever seen in his life came lumbering up to the bar.

"You the guy with the papers?"

And before RJ could answer, he said, "Let's go."

RJ thought to himself: this must be the one they call The Wolf. Or, as he must be known to his friends, Mr. Personality. My cruise mate.

As Lobo cast off the lines RJ thought that even though he theoretically sold them he had never actually ridden in one. Frankie always took care of that end. If there is ever a boat capable of doing a wheelie it will probably be a Cigarette Boat. It goes fast in neutral. Why is it that eighty or ninety miles an hour seems so much faster on water than on land? Thinking about a parachute was a stupid idea, of course, but it did occur to him. Did this thing have an ejection seat? I probably should have taken a ride in one of these things but somehow he had avoided that pleasure, he muses.

"Put this on."

RJ started to say, "You're kidding" but, was keenly aware that this man, undoubtedly, never kidded anyone…ever.

An impatient Lobo puts the black bag over his head.

Why was he so concerned about my being able to find this place again RJ wondered? How could you possibly find your way there in the first place? Nothing in any direction but mangrove covered islands each looking exactly like the last one. Birds get lost here.

RJ hadn't any idea how long they were screaming through the everglades; if they were in the everglades. He had absolutely no way on knowing where they were or which way they were heading.

Finally the boat slowed down and moments later the hood came off along with a small clump of RJ's hair.

"Ow! Hey, take it easy!"

"Sorry."

Yes, he actually said "sorry".

"Mr. de Benedetti is up at the big house. Follow the path and stay on it."

No one in his right mind would even think of straying from the trail, what there was of it. Water on either side. It had to be teeming with alligators or crocodiles or whatever they had around there. Snakes by the thousands no doubt. Spiders. Sharks. The works. Stray off the path? No chance. Feet don't fail me now.

Finally, a structure, something, appeared above the trees. As RJ got closer he was mildly amazed. Three, maybe four, stories high. Nothing on the first floor but the support stilts and what must have been the utilities cylinder. It looked, from where he stood, as if the bedrooms were on the second floor and the living quarters occupied the only part of the house that was above the trees. It was, he found out later, a fantastic view in all directions. Moreover, the damndest thing: the exterior of the top floor, be it the third or the fourth... it was hard to tell, gave the impression that the building was unoccupied... abandoned.

"How was the ride?"

"Only my laundry man knows how frightened I was."

He laughed. Whoever he was. And then appeared on the porch above RJ the sun at his back.

"Come on up. The elevator's on the other side of that column in front of you. I'll fix you a drink. Do you like rum?"

"Sure. Rum would be fine."

A house with an elevator in the middle of a swamp? How'd he get it here? He could hear Frankie, "Another of your stupid fucking questions. What difference does it make?"

RJ imagined that de Benedetti had to look like a backwoods version of Boris Karloff or Bela Lugosi, or maybe a machine gun toting Edward G. Robinson when you got up close. A scar was inevitable. A favourite comic book character from the forties sprang to mind. A German fighter pilot during world War Two who had crashed into the Everglades and emerged from the wreckage encrusted with vines and moss. He became the champion of free men everywhere ridding the world of the baddies and known to all as The Heap.

"I'm André de Benedetti. Welcome to my home."

"Thank you. Quite a place you've got here. I'm...."

"I know who you are, Mr. McCaw. I never have guests who just decide to drop in. I'm not fond of surprises. White rum with club soda and a squeeze of fresh lime. Very refreshing. I trust that will be acceptable."

"Yes, fine. Thank you. And please call me RJ"

"Of course and you may call me André. Let's sit on the veranda. There is usually a nice breeze at this time of day and the sunsets can be lovely here."

"Wherever we are."

"Yes, indeed. Wherever we are."

"I imagine it's a difficult place to find even once you've been here. Particularly if you've arrived with your head in a bag."

"I'm sorry about that little precaution. I hope you weren't too uncomfortable. Some people think I'm a little paranoid when it comes to my privacy."

"I can't understand where they'd get that idea."

"You're very quick, my young friend. I like that. You must stay the night. Today is my birthday and we're having a little get-together. You'll meet my wife and many of my friends."

"All wearing the same head-gear, no doubt. Don't they keep bumping into each other?"

André liked that one.

"No, really, thank you, I'm sorry I can't. I just came down here to get your signature on the contract and a few forms. I have to get back tonight."

"How are you going to do that? There are no planes, no helicopters, no cars and no roads. These waters are much too shallow and dangerous to try and navigate in the dark. And besides the Cigarette Boat is being wrapped."

"Wrapped?"

"Yes. It is my birthday present to my wife on my birthday."

"Nice. Nice touch. Nice present."

"My little backwoods boot-scooter gets bored easily. She wanted a little something to use to run up to South Beach. She likes to boogie, as she says, with her young friends. My wife comes from a little town in Louisiana called Grand Isle. Do you know it? Come to think of it, not much to know really. A few houses. A few bars. Not much else. Some of the oil companies base their drilling crews there. My wife's father was what they call a rough-roustabout. Spent his short life on the drilling platforms. Died in a fire when he was quite young. That's when I met Angeline, my wife. I represented the oil company in the litigation. When I met my future wife she was living with her recently widowed mother who was working, barefooted, in a restaurant that had a dirt floor. Some said the floor tasted better than the food.

I'd gone down there to try to settle some of the claims of the families that had lost relatives in the fire."

"You're a lawyer?"

"Was. I no longer practice the law. After close to thirty years of dealing with the Louisiana judicial system I finally had enough. The rig fire was the straw that broke the camel's back. I was also a pretty good defense se attorney in those days. I'm the third generation of de Benedetti's to practice criminal law in the state of Louisiana. There isn't an inmate in a Louisiana penal institution that doesn't know one of us de Benedettis.

At the time, there was some speculation that the fire, which resulted from an explosion, might not have been accidental. Seven men died. My client, the company that owned the rig, was convicted of the crime. The jury believed the fire was intentional in order to collect the insurance money. The company, a relatively small, independent operation, had been losing money and this particular hole was drying up. The trial and sub-sequent appeals took forever. The oil company eventually settled meager amounts on the families of the men who died. The experience also took away any desire I had to continue the practice of law. Well, enough of this morbid, depressing, discussion. Let's find you a place where you can relax for a while. Are you a napper?"

"A napper? Do I take naps?"

"Yes."

"Not since I was seven or eight."

"Too bad. Great for the system. I take a twenty or thirty minute nap every day. Lowers the blood pressure they tell me."

"You don't look like you need to worry about that."

"I'll take that as a compliment and thank you for it."

André led RJ down a circular stairway eschewing the elevator ("I've developed a little claustrophobia, since I had it installed.") to the second floor and deposited RJ in a very large and very comfortable bedroom. He thought, I've been in houses that were smaller than this room. Near the bed, neatly arranged on a small clothes rack, were several sets of outfits; jeans, western style shirts, underwear and socks. All his size. How'd he do that?

"Help yourself," André said.

RJ realized he certainly had to revise his initial impression of André de Benedetti. He didn't look like Karloff. Or Lugosi. Or even remotely like Edward G. Robinson. No one would ever confuse him with The Heap. Not short. Not particularly tall. Five nine or five ten. Maybe two hundred fairly firm pounds. Longish hair that was more pepper than salt. However, not a man that appeared to enjoy strenuous exercise.

It was not hard to imagine him wearing a light colored suit in an un air-conditioned courtroom, addressing a jury. Not an impressive figure at all until you were out of his presence and were unable to forget those eyes. Not the color, a nondescript gray, and not the size, which was no larger nor smaller than anyone else's. But, in a face that reflected a man who was calm and in total control, the eyes had an intensity that was inescapable. He was left with the distinct impression that, charming as he may be, André de Benedetti was not a man to have as an adversary. The boat ride had taken a lot out of RJ. Perhaps André was right; a short nap might be a good call.

RJ didn't know how long he slept, but it was a sleep of the deep, dark, restful variety. As he was coming out of it, the first thing he was aware of was the slight scent of wildflowers. Then there was the music. Cajun? Zydeco? He'd never known the difference. Sensing the presence of someone in the room he sat up and thought he saw the door that led to the hallway close.

RJ took a shower and put on one of the new outfits. It fit almost as well as Ginny's first husband's wedding tuxedo. He went downstairs and wandered into the kitchen.

"Everybody's outback on the barge. Mister de Benedetti said you're to join the party as soon as you wake up. My names Jolene. You need anything, you just ask me. Jolene was up to her elbows in some kind of a yellow, doughy mess."

"Thank you. What's that you're making?"

"Cornbread birthday cake. Mr. Andrés had the same cake every birthday of his life except when he was in the army. You be sure to get yourself a piece. You tell me what you think about cornbread birthday cake, you hear?"

"I'll look forward to it. Which way's the barge?"

"Out the front door and head toward the lights and the music. You can't miss it."

I wondered what Jolene would have looked like as a younger woman. She must have been spectacular. Six foot three if she was an inch. And skin any woman, or a lot of men, for that matter, would kill for. If you were casting an African princess in a movie, she'd get the part hands down; assuming your leading man was seven feet tall.

As RJ rounded a curve in the path, which for some reason seemed less intimidating at night than it was when he first arrived, the festivities were in full swing. In addition to the Cajun-Zydeco (whatever) band, there was a huge barbecuing something on a spit in a metal cooking contraption. Lots of smoke going straight up into the breezeless, moonlit sky.

There may have been two hundred people dancing, eating and drinking. All this on top of a big, flat barge that must have been towed in that afternoon because it wasn't there when he arrived in the early afternoon. Astounding what you can do with a lot of money.

"You missed seeing my present."

The faint scent of wildflowers.

"I'm Angeline. Everybody calls me Angel."

"And for good reasons, I'm sure."

"André said you were very quick."

"Who's to argue with the birthday boy?"

"He's tough to argue with even when it's not his birthday."

"I don't doubt that for a minute. How do you like the boat?"

"I love it. I can't wait to drive it, but André says I have to wait until tomorrow."

"What a spoilsport. He's right though. Better to see where you're going when you're travelling faster than the speed of light."

"How fast?"

"A slight exaggeration, perhaps."

"André asked me to tell you he has to go to Austin and Atlanta first thing in the morning. He probably won't even get to bed tonight. I'm going to take my new toy to Miami tomorrow and he says I'm to take you back with me."

"Be still my heart. This will be the longest night of my life."

"I think you're going to be my newest and best friend. Let's get something to drink. Are you hungry?"

"I just got up from a … I just got up."

He couldn't bring himself to say 'I had a nap.' Only children and old people took naps. He didn't want to appear to be either of these to this absolutely extraordinarily beautiful young woman.

"I think I'll wait on the food for a while. However, Jolene made me promise to try the birthday cake. And I don't think she's someone I'd like to cross."

"She's been looking after André since he was a baby."

"You're kidding. She can't be more than forty or forty-five!"

"Try seventy her next birthday. André says she may be the first person to live forever. He adores her. Can you dance?"

"Just lead me to the dance floor and call me Fred."

Prior to that night RJ would go to great lengths to avoid any semblance of dancing. Everyone in the world has something they don't do at all well. For him it was dancing. He always felt stiff and ill at ease on a dance floor. He'd convinced himself he was clumsy and uncoordinated. So, consequently, he was. However, much later that night he said to himself: I danced with more pretty women than I knew there were on the entire planet. I two stepped more two steps than I could count and drank more bottled beers than Harry and I consumed in our sojourns to Fat Jacks. And through it all I remained stone sober. Or, so he thought.

Somewhere around two in the morning André said he thought that since he was leaving so early in the morning it might be best if they conducted their business right then. Would RJ please collect his paperwork and meet him in his study in fifteen minutes.

He hated to leave the party. He'd almost forgotten why he was there. He'd promised himself one more dance with Angeline. He realized he couldn't call her Angel even though everyone else did. Angeline just seemed to fit her better. He also knew any hope of anything happening between the two of them was out of the question. She appeared to be happily married to a guy RJ thought to be, at a minimum, a shade sinister. But he also knew from that evening on he would always be a little bit in love with her.

He went back to his room, got Frank's briefcase, which he'd borrowed for the trip, and went downstairs. Stopping by the kitchen to see Jolene.

"Best cake I've ever had in my life. What was that frosting? It was like a combination of the world's richest chocolate ice cream combined with an incredible chocolate pudding."

"If you're a good boy I'll save a piece for you to take home with you."

"Thanks for everything. The food was terrific."

"You better get on now. Mister André is waitin' on you in his study."

Someone was putting me on about her being close to seventy.

"Have a seat. Would you like a drink?"

"Sure. Whatever you're having will be fine."

"Pacharon. Ever have it?"

"Maybe. Somewhere recently I think. Can't remember for sure. What's it called?"

"Pacharon. It's Basque. Made from a berry that only grows in northwestern Spain. Best served ice cold or on the rocks. Try it. If you don't like it I'll get you something else."

"That will be fine."

André quickly signed the sales contract and all the state and local documents without giving them more than a cursory glance. Being a lawyer he was undoubtedly familiar with them.

"How'd you like the party?"

"It was just great and from the sound of things it's still going strong."

"Sometimes my birthday soirees go on for days. Lots of these folks don't get out more than once or twice a year. When they do they make the most of it. I'm leavin' here in a couple of hours. Business. Angeline's takin' her new toy up to South Beach in the mornin'. She'll give you a ride back."

"Yes, she told me. That'll be just fine. Thank you ... for everything."

"Not at all. I appreciate you're comin' all the way down here."

"Wouldn't have missed it for the world. I mean that sincerely. I hope you'll invite me back some day."

"Well, now that you mention it, tell me somethin', just how enamored are you of the boat sellin' bidness?"

"It's a living. For now. I haven't really thought about it as a lifetime occupation."

"If you were going to have to make a commitment, in regards to the rest of your life, do you have an idea what you'd like to do?"

"I think I'd like to be a rich attorney with my own island. I'd like to be able to buy my wife two hundred and fifty thousand dollar toys."

"You would, would you? Be real sure. You know that old saying, "be careful what you wish for ... you just might get it.""

"I think it's a little late for me to be thinking about law school."

"I never did like practisin' the law. It wasn't what I had in mind for my life at all. I wanted to be the new Faulkner. Write the great important new novels of the

South. But, I fell in love with my high school sweetheart and by the time I was twenty we had two kids and another one on the way."

"I didn't know you'd been married before."

"Twice. Angeline's my third wife. Third time lucky, as they say. Third and last. If I had one wish, I'd wish I wasn't so much older than she is. She's a real incentive to take care of myself. And she keeps an eye on me as well. She see me drinkin' this stuff, she'd have my head for sure."

"One won't kill you."

"Never the less, the less said the better."

"Scout's honor."

Something that André just said saddened him and he appeared to sink into his own dark place. Maybe it was the age thing. RJ had the distinct impression that as far as he was concerned, RJ had left the room, leaving him to his own private rumination. The lull in the conversation vanished as quickly as it had materialized. However, when André reappeared, as it were, he was off on a completely new tangent of his own creation.

"I seem to have wasted so much time in the pursuit of the all mighty dollar. So much energy spent putting food into so many mouths. Now, that it is all over, my legal career, that is, I have so little to show for it. Two ex-wives that would put a gun to my head, if they had the chance. Three children I haven't seen in so long I don't know if I'd recognize them. I sometimes see families on television or in the movies … I still love the movies. I particularly like those Italian films. Black and white. Those people always huggin' and kissin' their kids. Do real people do that or just people in the movies? I suppose they do. I think that overt display of affection all began after my generation. I don't know."

"Look, André it's getting late and …"

"I don't respond well to interruption."

RJ felt that at that moment his body temperature dropped at least twenty degrees out of sheer fear.

"Sorry."

"But since you have been so rude and loutish it is incumbent upon you to redeem yourself by fetching us another drink."

He said this with a smile that was as cold as the ice RJ put into the glasses.

"Don't spare the ice. That's what my granddaddy always used to say."

RJ made the drinks and sat back down.

"Which is not to say that I didn't have some fun lawyerin'. Had some great times for sure and met some of the great crazies of these outrageous times. Met a man with half a lower jaw once in a parish courthouse not far from Baton Rouge. No idea what happened to his face. Frightening to look at. You know Baton Rouge means "red stick"? Why do you suppose they called it "red stick"? Got to make a note to look that up."

André leapt from his chair and on the way to his desk fell into my lap knocking my drink to the floor. I started to retrieve the now empty glass and spilled ice cubes.

"Leave it be. Help'll get it in the mornin'. Make yourself a fresh one."

He hadn't apologized. Maybe he was one of those guys who said they never cried and never said they were sorry.

RJ followed orders and poured another drink while his genial host made a note to himself on a legal pad printing very slowly with a felt pen.

"There. Now, where was I?"

"Baton Rouge. Some crazy guy with no jaw."

"Half a lower mandible and I didn't say he was crazy. What I said was … never mind. It's not important who he was or what he was. What is relevant is what he said."

André was back seated in a chair near RJ having replenished his drink on the way. A long night just started to look even longer.

In a very quiet voice…almost a whisper… as if in the telling of a secret he says, "This fella' says he knows who killed Jack Kennedy. 'Really, I say, who was it?' 'The Ku Klux Klan.' he says. 'Is that a fact,' I say. 'Plain as the nose on your face, if you can read the signs,' says he. 'Two Kennedy's and a King. K.K. K. What more of a clue do you need?' Some months later I happened to see one of those supermarket scandal sheets and here's this guy's picture on the front page – you can't miss that jaw line – and their callin' him a 'conspiracy theorist' and he's tellin' his story to the world. You figure. Who knows? My granddaddy used to say if 'you can't disprove it, don't disbelieve it'."

His eyes started to cloud over as he passed on to another time. Maybe he was fishing with his grandfather. He tipped his head back and his mouth fell open. RJ got out of his chair and moved toward him to take his drink before it too fell to the carpet. A miscalculation on his part. André stirred. RJ was able to sit back down just as André shot back up fully awake, well almost, and ready for more conversation. More monologue would be closer to actuality.

"There commenced a time recently in my life … the 'filthy fifties' I call it … when, on occasion, I saw new versions of old faces from the past … modern day reincarnations of former friends and loved ones. Not exact look-a-likes, but close, real close. I saw an elderly man just the other day and I said to myself "Why, that's that crazy old Cajun Louis Camp." But it can't be, of course, 'cause poor Louie's been dead now … let's see … well … a long time."

André drifts off again, but only briefly.

"I had a bodyguard years ago we called "The Gripper". That was back in the days when I was involved in some pretty heavy law suits against the oil companies, after Angeline and I had married, and I was gettin' some pretty serious soundin' threats and a bodyguard seemed like a real good idea. Anyway, the story was that Nunzio – that was his real name, Nunzio Coraldi – had gotten into a brawl in New Orleans with a little sweetheart known to friend and foe alike as "Snuffy". You can imagine how he came by that moniker. Moniker? I haven't used that word in twenty years. Maybe more. Moniker. Strange. Where was I?"

"The Gripper."

"Right. Anyway one of them said somethin' the other took umbrage with and they headed out of the bar onto the street. Someone had the temerity to call the local constabulary, who when they arrived found The Gripper "snuffed," as it were, and an alive but unconscious Snuffy. He came to work for me after he'd gotten out of prison. I had to let him go after a short time; his presence was just too intimidating. He even scared me and I'm fearless, as my friend Oklahoma Whitey used to say.

I ran into him a year or so ago in a Cuban nightclub in Miami. I can't remember what I was doin' there. Well, yes I do, but it's not germane to our conversation of this evening. It was back in the days when I thought I was the world's champion bourbon drinker and set out to prove it each and every night.

93

He, Snuffy, was workin' as a doorman and bouncer in this place. A Cuban Mafioso by the name of Tato owned it. Casa Tato. Casa del Tato. Somethin' like that. I forget. The story was that he he'd come by the money to buy this place by doing a little job on some drug runner who'd gotten a little fast and loose with the profits from a cocaine deal. When they found this unfortunate hombre he was hangin' by his ankles on a fishing pier with his severed right hand stuffed into his mouth and held there with a piece of duct tape. He was still alive. They say Tato bribed a cop and got the hand which he had freeze-dried like coffee and mounted on a plaque. He had it on display in his office at the club. Sort of a warning to others, I suppose. What made me think of that, I wonder? I got to call Cracker Graham … ain't that a name, and it's his real one too. I got to ask him about that 'red stick' bidniss. He'll know. Cracker's from that part of Louisiana. He had the audacity to accept a football scholarship to the University of Michigan after he had practically been handed the starting quarter-backs job at L.S.U. His daddy never did forgive him. 'Specially after he almost took Michigan to the Rose Bowl."

"André if you'll excuse me," RJ said as he got up as if to leave.

"You haven't learned a thing. I don't respond to that. I'm not finished with you. Sit down. Please."

Incurring his wrath any further didn't seem like a real good idea. He sat.

"On a man's birthday it is important for him to take stock of his life and contemplate his accomplishments and plans for the future. In addition I want you to consider your own future and how it might cohabit with mine. That's not such an unpleasant thought is it?"

"No, sir," he lied, "not at all."

RJ's eyelids were getting very heavy and he was starting to see double. If only he could just lie down for a few minutes. "Do you have a dog, Jack?"

"A dog? No, sir, I sure don't."

"I have a dog, Jack. His name is Thor. A big, black Lab. Smartest dog I ever met."

"I don't remember seeing a dog...."

"He's at the vet's in Atlanta. He has to die. He's very old. Hip dysplasia and arthritis. Has a very difficult time standing up. Angeline says we should have him put to sleep. I can't do that. Could you? Could you make out a check while your dog was being gassed or given some kind of injection in the next room?"

"I would think that would be very difficult, sir.

Please don't call me sir, Jack. I'm not that old. Or maybe I am. They say having an old, sick pet is preparation for your own mortality and the deaths of people you care for."

He seemed, once again, to be drifting away; lost in his own thoughts. Maybe he'd finally fall asleep. Fat chance.

"There ought to be another way to deal with an old pet. I feel like I should take him for a long walk and shoot him myself. But I don't know if I could do that. If I ever wanted someone killed Snuffy said, rather matter of factly, that he would do it for me... free of charge. His way of thanking me for negotiating his early release from prison. Wonder if he'd kill?"

"Did he really mean it, that he would actually kill someone for you?"

"Oh, yes. Definitely. No question about it. Sent a shiver through my whole body the way he said it. He might even get great pleasure from it. Wouldn't surprise me one bit. I'm sure when he snuffed The Gripper it made him intensely happy. However, I might be all wrong. He's a hard man to read. Never smiles. Rarely, if ever, shows any emotion. The man is nuttier than homemade cake. You got someone you want killed, Jack?"

"No. No. Of course not. I was just ... you know ... wondering."

"Yes, I know. I do understand; you were just 'wonderin'."

"Right."

"Ever just 'wonder' if you could kill someone. Jack? Not in combat. Not to protect a wife or a child, but just kill someone because you thought they truly needed killin'? Ever think about that, Jack."

"No, I don't believe I have."

"You're a liar Jack and that is for sure. Ain't a grown man alive that hasn't thought about killin' someone, sometime, and most of us have thought about it more than once. A bully, perhaps? A rival? Someone that stood in your way in a deal that could make you wealthy for the rest of your life? An ex-wife? Surely there must be someone you'd like to have killed at one time or another."

An ex-wife? Why had he said that? It had to be a wild guess.

RJ had to get some air. He bolted for the French doors and threw myself outside on the veranda. Someone was singing some song that sounded like "Joe Lee Blond." Made no sense. He slugged up several huge breaths and went back into Andrés study. He'd been saved. André was gone.

RJ somehow managed to make it back to his room and was naked by the time he hit the bed face down. At some point just before he passed out he thought he heard a helicopter overhead.

Minutes later somebody slapped hard on his bare bottom.

"Wakie, wakie, sunshine. Time to have at it."

"What? It had to be the middle of the night. Someone was in his room, had hit him on the butt and was opening the shades and letting in the blinding sun."

"Nine-thirty. There's a tray with some breakfast and hot coffee. Miss Angeline says you're leavin' in one hour and don't be late. She wants to be in Miami by one."

"Jesus, Jolene, I'm not even dressed."

"I noticed that. How you feeling' this morning? You and Mister André have a nice little chat, did you?"

"Mostly, I listened."

"He has a nephew, also a lawyer, worked for Mister André for a while. I heard him say he was in a meetin' once, that lasted over eight hours, and Mister André was the only one talked the entire time. Don't ever try interruptin' him when he's on a roll either."

"So I found out."

"I'll leave you now. You need anything?"

"Like maybe plasma you mean?"

"You have some of that black coffee and those eggs with hot sauce and you'll be fine."

Eggs with hot sauce. No way. He promised himself no more booze. Not ever? No, never.

He somehow managed to take a shower and get dressed. Shaving was out of the question without an emergency medical team standing by. If he attempted to bend over he got very dizzy. He raised his feet over his head one at a time while lying on his back and in that position was able to tie his shoes. He managed to gag down some coffee, half a piece of toast and stumbled downstairs.

Jolene had called up from the kitchen to say Angeline was already on the boat and he should get down there right away. He found his way to the kitchen and said his good-byes to Jolene who handed him a small box tied with a ribbon.

"Where's Mr. de Benedetti?"

"Somewhere, but not here. Never even went to bed." "He and Lobo are long gone. Big, important business."

He hobbled down to the dock as quickly as he could, given the circumstances. Angeline was onboard the Cigarette Boat and the engine was running. Exhaust smell. Gag.

"Good morning."

"That's one opinion."

"How're you feeling?"

"I'll let you know if and when I survive."

"You don't look so good."

"I'm fine. Light green is my natural skin color."

"Fresh air will do you good."

"Promise?"

And with that they were off. If he hadn't had a seat belt on he would have been catapulted overboard. What fun. The blindfold didn't help. Yeah, he had to wear it again. It's a wonderful thing, paranoia.

Had his stomach not been threatening to launch a green rocket at any given moment and had his head not been throbbing to the rhythm of Gene Krupa's "Sing, Sing, Sing" drum solo, it would have been a great day. Angeline let him take off the hood after they were clear of "the compound" as she called it. Clear, cloudless sky. About eighty degrees. The air smelled clean and fresh. The water was as still as glass.

They traveled for about an hour at something just short of mach one. Angeline handled the boat very well keeping, as RJ could tell by the position of the sun, to a fairly easterly course. Turning sharply sometimes to avoid an object in the water. He was feeling better and worse at the same time. His head had stopped aching, but his stomach, on the other hand, didn't like the strong coffee. Chicory, maybe. Just don't let me get sick and embarrass myself, he prayed.

Angeline seemed impervious to his discomfort and concentrated entirely on enjoying her new toy. If she got something this expensive on Andrés birthday RJ wondered, what would he give her on her own birthday? He'd probably never know for he was sure he was going to die this very day; maybe in a manner of minutes. Man was not born to travel this fast. Not on land and certainly not on the water. And then, miraculously, the boat slowed.

"You look like you could use a beer. Or a stomach pump. Or both. Let's try a beer first."

Moments later they dropped anchor about a hundred shallow yards from a beach and waded ashore. The water was gin clear and pleasantly warm. They walked up to a little restaurant that looked like it had been there since Christ was a corporal. A sign advertised 'the coldest beer in the keys.' Didn't they all?

They got a couple of long necks and sat on the deck looking out at the boat.

"That thing looks fast just sitting there."

"I love it. I absolutely love it."

"Does it make you crazy sitting here with a sick drunk when you could be terrorizing half the other boats in the bay?"

"I can do that later. They'll always be there. Right now it's nice sitting here with you. What a gorgeous day. Makes you want to live forever."

"Right now I'll settle for surviving the next hour and if I don't feel any better soon I'll elect the suicide route."

"You'll be fine. Have another beer."

And she was right, of course, eventually he began to come around. Not up to hundred yards sprints, but definitely improved.

And the better he felt the more attractive Angeline became. Hard to imagine since she was already the most spectacular looking woman on the planet.

What did she see in André he wondered? Other than several million dollars, his own island and power, power, power, what did he have? Maybe they had a Svengali and Trilby thing going. Whatever he had it must have been substantial. There was no denying it; once you met him you weren't likely to soon forget him.

"Where's André off to?"

"Austin and then Atlanta, I think. He had a seven am meeting.""

"It's none of my business, but how can a normal human being attend a seven a.m. meeting when he hasn't had any sleep?"

"You may have noticed that André is no normal human being. Far from it. And he needs very little sleep. He probably took a nap while Lobo flew the helicopter. He sometimes goes two or three days without any sleep at all. Like just before he retired, when he was working on an important custody case, he worked all night for five straight days. Telephoned people at two or three o'clock in the morning. Drove his staff crazy. Then when the trial was over he slept the better part of a week."

"Can't be very good for his health."

"It's not. And that's one of the reasons he doesn't do it anymore. Today is an exception. I don't know what it is about but whatever it is it's making him very uncharacteristically anxious."

"A big deal?"

"I guess so. Ever since he officially stopped practicing the law he doesn't discuss his business with me."

"He doesn't practice law at all anymore? What does he do?"

"I don't really know. If you ask him he'll say he is an expediter."

"What does he expedite?"

"Ask him."

"I have the distinct impression from talking with him last night in his study that his answer wouldn't be terribly revealing. Charming, mesmerizing, but not particularly informative."

"See, you know him better than you think you do."

"Which is to say not at all. He offered me a job, I think."

"Really? Doing what?"

"Well, that's the thing. I don't know. 'A position with responsibilities to be determined at a later date,' was the way he put it. Or something like that. My recollections of last night are a bit foggy."

"Are you going to take it…whatever it is?"

"I told him I'd think about it. I'm not in love with the boat business, even though you do meet the most fascinating people."

"Thank you."

"You're welcome. Before I make any decisions regarding employment I have some personal business that needs taking care of. Then we'll see. And of course I'd want to know more about what André wants from me. I don't want to work for him just because he likes to have me around. What happens if and when he decides he no longer does?"

"You think that is a distinct possibility?"

"Don't you?"

"Yes and no. André can be very capricious and yet few men are more loyal. Lobo's been with him forever.

But Lobo fulfills a definite need, I would guess. Like keeping the boss in one piece."

"Not always an easy job."

"I'm sure. André seems like he could be a little abrasive at times."

"You could say that, but don't say it to Lobo. He doesn't take kindly to slurs against the boss."

"But, other than that, he's a great guy to be with. A real fun seeker our Lobo. I noticed that right away."

The beer was finally making him feel almost human.

"Are you hungry? Do you think you could hold down lunch?"

"Absolutely. I'm starved. What shall we have?"

"Do you want to stay here or go somewhere else?"

"It's your neighborhood. Oh shit!"

"What's the matter?"

"Jolene gave me a piece of birthday cake to take home. I forgot all about it. I must have left it on the pier. Oh, damn it!"

RJ is rummaging through his pockets.

"Now what?"

"My car keys. Oh, right. They're with my car in Marathon. At a place called Smitty's…Smelly's…"

"Sweaty's."

"Right."

"Don't worry. I'll drop you off there."

"I'm a little concerned about the car."

"Don't be. Sweaty's an old friend of Andrés. Safe as Fort Knox."

They ended up at a little sea food place on another key. More beer and fresh shrimp and conch gazpacho.

"Is André at all like his father?"

"Why do you ask that?"

"Just curious, I guess. It seemed like a natural question in as much as…"

"I never met his father. He died when André was twelve. A drilling rig accident."

"A drilling rig accident? What was a …"

"He caught himself just in time, he hoped."

"What was a what?"

"What was a what?" Did you really say 'what was a what?'

"Yes, you jerk. What were you going to say?"

"Nothing, really. I have to go to the head."

André said his father was a lawyer. Three generations of lawyers, he'd said. RJ wanted to ask Angeline about André's grandfather, but he couldn't figure out a way to do it tactfully; so he just let the subject drop. It made him wonder though: why would he lie to me? What did he have to gain or was it just some strange insecurity quirk about having a laborer for a father rather than a professional. He'd never find out.

When returned to the table he said, "Another thing that seems kinda' weird. Last night he kept calling me Jack."

Angeline laughed and said, "One of his quirks. He calls peoples by the names he thinks they should have rather than the ones they actually have. How about that, Jackie?"

Later in the afternoon Angeline dropped him off at Sweaty's. He hated to see this day end.

Towards sunset RJ arrived back at the boatyard where Frankie was over joyed at seeing him.

"Where the fuck have you been?"

"I was invited to spend the night. His birthday party and everything just took longer than you thought it would."

"You get all that shit signed?"

"No problem. It's all in your briefcase."

"Tell me somethin'. What's his house like?"

"Nice. Three stories. Tastefully decorated. He owns his own key. At least I think it's a key. Seems more like a combination of a key and a glade. Very isolated. I couldn't really see very much. Most of the time I was there it was dark."

"Sounds more like those houses that used to be in the Everglades before the hurricane of '49 blew them all away. That's when the government decided not to let the owners rebuild and turned the whole area into some kinda' park."

"Yeah, well there's still one house down there someplace. They made me wear a blindfold going in and out of the place."

"You're kidding."

"Really, no joke. Tell me something, do you know what de Benedetti does for a living these days?"

"Not really. He used to be a big shot lawyer, as you know. Then he got into some kind of trouble in Louisiana or Alabama and got his license lifted. I don't know what he's into now. You used to see his picture in the papers all the time when he was practicing law. Haven't heard a thing about him in years. Except, there was a story going around a year or two ago… some guy was in the process of writing a story about him … what do you call it?"

"An unauthorized biography?"

"Yeah, that's it. I remember 'cause the day after the story come out in the paper de Benedetti was here on one of his semi-annual 'just lookin around' jaunts. The paper said the title of the book was, Out of Order: The Unauthorized Biography of André de Benedetti. I asked André how he felt about having some guy writing a book about him.

"What'd he say?"

"He said he thought it would be an interesting read and he hoped the guy lived long enough to finish it. And he said it without crackin' a smile."

"You ever hear about the book being released?"

"Not a word. 'Course I ain't much into the book section of the Sunday paper. You look a little tired."

"That's funny, I feel exhausted."

"Yeah, well it's been slower than shit the last two days. Why don't you take off the rest of the day. Get some sleep."

"Bless you, my son. I'll do that. See you tomorrow."

When he got back to his apartment the building manager had left him a note from Harry taped to the door asking him to call. Later, he told himself, right now I need sleep.

He hoped he'd dream of Angeline. It didn't happen. He had, once again, one of those dreamless sleeps that allows one to cleanse the mind and awaken well rested. He was beginning to become a believer in this nap business. He awoke about seven-thirty that evening and called Harry.

"Where you been, boy? I've missed you. Seems like I haven't seen you in weeks."

"It has been awhile, hasn't it? I've been working long hours at the boat yard. A couple of guys are on vacation. And I had to go to the Keys for a couple of days. How's your golf game?"

105

"If I could putt I'd be on the tour. Unfortunately, I can't putt worth a damn. Maybe I need a new putter."

"Maybe you need a different instructor."

"Not so. The boy's a genius. Very concise. Doesn't confuse you with a lot of jargon and complicated theories. I think I need a new putter, that's all."

"So you said. How's the mother of the 'genius'? Are you making any headway?"

"That's another story, best told in person. How about a drink?"

"Fine. How's about I meet you at Jack's in an hour."

"Perfect."

RJ took the world's longest shower, shaved and got dressed. He was starting to have the nucleus of a plan and was eager to discuss it with Harry.

"I had dinner with Chase the night before last. That's why I left the message for you. He's very concerned about his mother and at the same time he is barely able to conceal his loathing for her. According to Chase, his mother's cocaine habit is out of control and she has been hanging out with some very unsavory types from the Miami area. Sound familiar? Chase says there have been complaints to the police from Ginny's neighbors about late night parties, loud music and skinny dipping in the pool; which is clearly visible, as you know, from a number of homes in the neighborhood."

"Terrific."

"I expected a reaction from you, however, 'terrific' was not what I would have guessed."

"What you're telling me is exactly what I have thought about Ginny for years. She's out of control. She's a menace to anyone who comes in contact with her and it's time she went bye-bye... permanently."

"Bye-bye?"

"Died, Harry, died. It's time to say adios to the wicked witch of the south. Or north. Or whatever the fuck you called her."

"I'm not sure what you're getting at, but if I had an inkling I'd think it might be a tad extreme. What about just having her committed? You know, locked up somewhere where she can't do any harm to herself or anyone else."

"And how are we going to do that? 'Hello, I'm the ex-husband of the woman in question and even though I haven't had any significant personal contact with her I have been spying on her and I can guarantee you she's nuts and ought to be put away.'"

"I don't know what you have in mind but the whole scheme is a bit off the wall, isn't it. I mean you're going to have to carry this burden of responsibility for the rest of your life. Is it worth it? Have you seriously considered the implications of your actions? Has it occurred to you that you might be giving Ginny and this situation too much domination over your own life? Mightn't you be better served by just wrapping the whole thing in a bunch of roses, wishing it the best and letting the whole thing go?"

"That's a nice idea, Harry. Nicely said. Almost poetic. But, if there was ever a question in my mind, there is a little plot of land a few short miles from here, that by its very presence, erases all traces of doubt from my mind."

"Your daughter's grave."

"That's right. I've said it before and I'll say it again: there are no accidents. That bitch changed my life forever and she's not going to get away with it. I've wasted too much time already. There is a very short list of things in my life that I am absolutely sure of and this is numero uno."

"Do you truly believe she is personally responsible for the death of you daughter?"

"Where the hell have you been, Harry? When Callie drowned there were four people in the house. Three adults and a child. And while we're on the subject how about that father of hers. Here's a guy who has more money than Croesus, buys his daughter and grand-daughter a house and yet there was no alarm system in the pool. So who's accountable? You tell me. The maid, the drug addled boyfriend, or the mother?"

"Now, look …"

"No, you look. I'm not finished. Let's not forget that when Callie died Ginny was trying to keep me from seeing her ever again. And why? Was I a bad influence? No. Was I planning on harming the child in some way? Come on. Did I try to stop Ginny from moving with the child to Florida? No. All I wanted was to be able to see my daughter and have some say in how she was raised. That's all. But, for my many transgressions, whatever they might have been, I had to be punished."

"All right. You've made you point."

"Again."

"Yes, again. So, that being decided, now what?"

"I suppose that depends on you. This might be the point where you say, 'thank you very, much but I've had enough'."

"I've come this far. I'll play out the hand. I also have my own reasons for wanting to be involved. I hate to see what all this might do to the boy. He's really a nice kid, but he has a lot of anger. He told me something that I hesitate to tell you."

"Go ahead. After what's happened I can't imagine anything worse."

"Chase strongly believes that Ginny has had sex with her father."

"What! Are you serious?"

"Chase, fortunately, didn't offer any particulars."

"And you believe him?"

"You should have seen the look on his face when he told me. He is in great pain with the situation and I believe he had to tell someone just to get it off his chest and I guess he trusts me enough…."

"Jesus Christ! What next? I…I started to say I can't believe this, but…. Look, Ginny, as long as I've known her, has had what might be called a passing acquaintance with the truth. If there are two ways of relating an anecdote, say, and one was the truth of the matter and the other was a more interesting, or funnier way of relating it she would always choose the later. For instance, listen to this. One night after a few pops Ginny told me about life with dear old dad. Seems he liked to send her stuff; mostly expensive clothes. Ginny told me that up in the attic in her mother's house…no wait. That's not right. I'm confusing myself. She actually took me to her mother's attic and showed me the evidence of his largess, as it were. Rack after rack of all assorts of stuff. Most of which still had the sales slips attached. Then another day shortly before we married her mother took us to the basement where there were, I kid you not, barrels of sterling silver. It looked like Tiffany's had moved to Illinois. She wanted us to move them to our house. Get them out of her way. Anyway, back to the story telling evening in regard to Dorsey. Ginny told me a story I have a hard time believing. She and Dorsey had gone to Paris. One night they went a ways out of town to an old mansion that had been converted to a nightclub of sorts called The Circus. When I say 'of sorts' it was actually all things to do with sex. Live participation by guests was encouraged. Not that they needed to be coerced. I'll not go into the details. Suffice it to say both

109

she and her father joined in. So, now this whole current sex with daddy business doesn't seem out of the realm of possibility. However, as far as I'm concerned it doesn't make a particle of difference. I'm still going to try my damnedest to drive her off the planet."

"All right, so be it. Now the question is: how do we go about it? I, for one, haven't the foggiest idea."

"I do. We get someone else to do it."

"Yes, of course, but whom? I don't number hired killers in my list of friends."

"I heard of a man when I was in the Keys who may be able to help us come to grips with our problem. André mentioned him and it wasn't until later when something clicked in and I remembered having come across him. And get this: his name is Snuffy."

"Snuffy? As in…."

"Exactly. I sorta' knew him when I was a kid growing up outside Chicago. Even though we lived in roughly the same part of town, I knew him mostly from the stories. He worked for one of Al Capone's lawyers. Looked after the kids. Drove them to school. Odd jobs. Gardener. Whatever needed to be done."

"Would that included killing someone?"

"Maybe. Yesterday I called a cop I knew in Chicago. Asked him what he knew about Snuffy these days. Said I was writing a Capone story. Needed some background. Might want to interview him. He told me Snuffy left town when both Capone and his lawyer died. The cop said he'd heard from someone who saw him that Snuffy was working as a bouncer in Miami. A joint called Taco's or Tayto's…something like that."

Later that evening after having looked up the address in the Yellow Pages RJ drove to South Beach to a bar called Tato's Place or rather what was left of it. A fire

110

had pretty much gutted the building leaving only the burnt out neon sign that read TAT ACE.

Before driving back home RJ decided to get something to eat at a little mom and pop restaurant across from what was left of Casa Tato. It looked like one of those places that serve good food for a reasonable price. He sat at the bar and ordered some plantains, a small salad, and roasted chicken. While Pop was pouring him a Red Stripe beer he asked what had happened to the place across the street.

"Fuego. Big fire. Somebody sent in a flaming faggot and he burned it to the ground."

Mom intercedes and says, "Don't pay no attention to him, senor. Hector, clean up that booth in the corner. He's not a bad guy. Just has a stupid sense of humor."

She gave Hector a slap on the back of the head and in the process spilled RJ's beer.

"Gaw dam it! See what you made me do." She brought RJ a fresh bottle and while she was wiping up the spill he noticed that although she was barely five feet tall she had the biggest hands he had ever seen in his life. This old couple reminded RJ of a friend of his who once said that his parents were so weird that he hoped he was adopted.

"How did it really happen…the fire?" he asks her.

"Chew an insurance guy? You look like an insurance guy."

"Do I? I don't know how to take that. No, I'm not. I sell boats. I'm looking for the guy who I think owned the place. Friend of mine from Chicago. Got a funny name."

"Snuffy!"

"Yeah, that's him. He really a friend of yours?"

"Long time ago. Just wanted to look him up. Say hello."

"Do jew know Islas Canarias the restaurant?"

111

"Cuban place?"

"Dat's it. You going to look for him?"

"I think so."

"Be careful. He might not be the same guy you knew in Chicago. He a changed man since this place burned down. I hear he drinks too much and has a bad temper. Not that he was all that pleasant before. My stupid husband was in there one night and had too much to drink hi'sef. When he gets like that he thinks he's Jose Louis of some other tough guy. I forget. Anyway, Snuffy asks him to leave and Hector tries to pick a fight with him. Bad idea. Berry bad idea. Snuffy picks him up, carries him over his head to the front door and tosses him out into the middle of the street. Hector is lucky there was a lot of traffic that night and it was moving berry slow. Anyway, Hector just misses getting run over and Snuffy yells at him, Hey Hector, you know what. You don bounce so good. That was the last time he went in there."

RJ had some trouble finding the Islas Canarias as a large tropical storm had blown in from the Caribbean and made seeing difficult. When he finally found the place it was packed and there was a waiting line outside. RJ managed to talk himself onto a stool in the bar. After about two hours he decided Snuffy wasn't going to show up and he elected to head home. On the way out of the restaurant he happened to ask the woman who was taking names at the entrance if she knew if Snuffy would be coming in later.

"That's him right there at the small table in the corner. The guy with the hat."

RJ hadn't seen this guy come in. Anyway he didn't look like the Snuffy he remembered. He was wearing an old gray suit that look liked it had gone out of style right after the war. He had half a loaf of bread in one hand and was attacking a bowl of soup with the other as if he hadn't eaten in a week. He appeared to needed a shave and a bath and he looked about as dangerous as a butterfly.

RJ decided to wait until he had finished eating and left the restaurant before he tried talking to him.

Who knew what his reaction would be when RJ explained what he had in mind. The fewer witnesses to their talking the better. When Snuffy finally paid and headed to the door RJ followed shortly thereafter.

Snuffy was half way down the block before RJ saw him. For a big man he moved effortlessly although he had a slight limp. His walk reminded RJ of a fierce looking alley cat he'd seen on a street in San Juan, Puerto Rico years ago. Even though the cat had only three and a half legs and appeared to have only one eye RJ, for a moment, seriously considered taking him back to Chicago, cleaning him up and having a patch made for the missing eye and having him fit for a peg leg.

Catching up to Snuffy RJ said, "Excuse me."

Turning around Snuffy growled, "What the fuck do you want?"

Hardly an auspicious beginning.

"If I could just have a minute of you time."

"You've already had a minute. Fuck off."

As they were crossing the street in the still falling rain a cab came around a corner and skidded to as top inches from both men. Snuffy hit the hood of the car with his fist leaving a good-sized dent. The driver started to get out of the taxi but though better of it after seeing the dent and a quick look at Snuffy. He quickly put the car in gear and sped away.

Snuffy turned to RJ looked him over and said, "Coffee."

"Sure, yeah, coffee would be fine."

"Who ask you?"

They went to a dank little smoke filled coffee house on a dreary side street. Snuffy pointed to the coffee machine and said "Espresso doble." At least that's what RJ thought he said. He was petrified that he would order the wrong thing. When he paid and put the coffees on the table Snuffy didn't rip his arm out of the shoulder socket or throw scalding coffee in his face so he figured he had heard correctly. They sat sipping, or rather in Snuffy's case slurping their coffees for what to RJ seemed hours with no words spoken.

"So, what do you want?"

"I thought we might talk a little business."

"Business."

"Yeah."

"Your business or my business?"

"Well, actually, your business."

"And just what business is that?"

"I beg your pardon."

"You deaf? What business is it you think I'm in, you dumb fuck?"

"Uh, oh."

"Ah, well, I was led to believe…"

"Oh, yeah. Who by?"

"Who by? Ah, well…"

"You want somebody killed."

"No, well, yes, actually that's…that's it. I ah, want someone put out…"

"You pay for theses coffees?"

"Ah, yes."

"Let's go."

And with that Snuffy walked out of the coffee bar and immediately turned into the dark, garbage-strewn alley with RJ close behind. Suddenly, the big man turns with unimaginable speed, grabs RJ by the throat, lifts him straight up into the air and slams him into a brick wall. With his free hand he begins emptying RJ's pockets. Wallet, cash, car keys. Dropping them on the ground and finally releasing RJ.

"You don't have much money here."

RJ croaks, "I never carry a lot of cash in case...."

"Ten thousand."

"Ten thousand?"

"You deaf? Ten thousand dollars."

"That's what it costs?"

"Here."

Snuffy hands RJ his wallet and car keys. "I'm keepin' the cash for my time. So, you got ten grand? I don't think so."

"No, but I can get it."

Harry would come through. He was sure of it.

"Yeah, when?"

"When would you need it?"

"Tomorrow."

"Ah, tomorrow?"

Snuffy laughs and then says, "When do you need this person...removed?"

"I don't know. I hadn't thought about. I don't have a schedule."

"So, you tell me when and where this person lives. You give me the money...cash...small bills... and I do the dirty deed."

"Just that simple."

"Exactly. So, tell me, this person got a name?

"I don't want to tell you her name right now."

"Her."

And with that Snuffy turns and quickly walks down the alley.

"Hey, wait a second. Where are you going? How will I find you?"

Without slowing in down or turning around Snuffy yells, "No deal."

"Hey, what's the matter?"

"You figure it out."

Harry has installed a putting green in the backyard and is practicing his stroke. RJ enters through the side gate.

"Looks pretty good."

Harry, not sure of the relationship after their last encounter, is a bit chary.

"Getting there. Where have you been, old stain?"

"I've been busy working. And I drove down to Miami."

"Oh, and…"

"Ah, I looked around. Couldn't find him."

"I see. Oh, well it might be for the best."

"This is new."

"Putting seems to be the weakest part of my game."
"Thought my own putting green might help. So far it hasn't made an appreciable difference."

"Maybe you need a new instructor."

Harry's reaction is a tad too quick and strong.

"Not so. The boy's a genius. Maybe I need a new putter."

"By the way, Chase tells me he's very concerned about his mother. Says her cocaine habit is…"

"Cocaine habit?"

"Hmm. How much do you know about your former stepson's life?"

"Very little. Why?"

"Did you know he graduated with honors from the University of Miami? Wanted to be a doctor. But when it came time for medical school his mother balked at coming up with the money. Told him if he wanted med school he could pay for it himself."

"What? That woman or her father could buy a whole fucking hospital if they wanted to."

"Pretty much sums up Chase's opinion as well."

"Except her attitude seems to have pushed him to the point of other more drastic and far-reaching measures."

Harry pauses to try a rather short putt ... "that he misses."

"Damn. It seems, as an underclassman, Chase did a little experimenting with some very high power and potentially dangerous drugs himself."

"God..."

"He managed to acquire enough knowledge of the world's common and uncommon narcotics, some of which come closer to being poisons than drugs, to qualify as something of an expert."

"Did he become addicted?"

"No, he quit in time, but along the way he managed to turn his mother into being totally dependent on him for her supply."

"You won't give me the money for medical school ... I'll get it out of you another way."

"Precisely."

"Where did you hear all this?"

"My friend at the club."

RJ thinks about this for a while as Harry lines up another putt.

"Yeah, well, I'm dropping the whole thing. I'm not going to screw up my life trying to ... I'm not even sure what it is I'm trying to do. I think I'll give it up for Halloween."

This gets Harry's attention away from his putting.

"Speaking of which, herself is having a Halloween party. Interested in going?"

"Oh, absolutely. Wouldn't miss it."

"I'm at a complete loss as to what to wear."

"Has there ever been some really frightening golfer?"

"Some ogre who beat his victims to a bloody pulp with a sand wedge? Or, better yet, a mashie. You know, Harry the Chipper?"

"That is truly awful."

"Thank you."

RJ is having a cup of coffee and a piece of toast on the balcony of his condo. He looks across the causeway and observes Ginny and a trainer working out.

Ginny finishes her workout, and while her trainer is packing up, she takes off her sweats and dives into the pool bare-assed naked. It does not escape RJ's attention, or the trainer's, that Ginny is still in great shape. The trainer waves good-bye as he leaves. Ginny swims a few laps, gets out of the pool, grabs a towel, and heads into the house. RJ watches for a moment more, finishes his coffee and stares into space.

Early evening. RJ and Frankie are walking out of the office.

"I appreciate your locking up. I gotta' run."

"No problem. See you tomorrow."

Frankie drives off. RJ proceeds towards the boats flashlight in hand. It is very still on the water. Not even a hint of a breeze and it is very quiet. For no apparent reason RJ stops and listens intently. Nothing. RJ continues checking out each boat. Something at the far end of the pier makes a small splash. As he nears the dark water there is another splash on the ocean side of the last yacht a sail boat. Fish? Alligators? RJ climbs on board and walks forward leaning over the side trying to see what made the noise. Suddenly from behind him someone in an all black wet suit wraps a line around his neck. The person hits RJ in the kidney while holding on to the rope. The force of the blow knocks RJ to his knees where the line is momentarily loosened, but only for a split second. The line becomes tight once again and RJ is being hoisted up the mast. He struggles to free himself, but he is slowly losing consciousness. His body is almost to the top of the mast when a strong light flashes on the scene. It is the security cop.

"Hey, what's going on down there?"

The person in black lets go of the line. RJ comes crashing to the deck. The intruder slides into the water and disappears. The cop runs toward RJ.

"RJ, are you okay?"

RJ can barely get his breath let alone speak. Just what he needs; another assault on his vocal cords.

Harry and RJ exit the clinic and walk towards Harry's car. RJ is limping slightly and carries a prescription bag.

"You should go to the police about this and that shooting business."

RJ croaks, "Yeah, right. Well, officer, I often take my new gun and go target shooting in the middle of nowhere. And I don't know what happened, but someone started shooting at my empty Coke bottles and then at me. Do you know who it was? Yes, it was my ex-father-in-law."

"Listen RJ…"

"And then when that didn't work he decided to run me up the mast like a goddam spinnaker. No, I didn't get a look at him either time, but I know it was him: I recognized his scent. English Leather."

RJ is sitting having a drink. He is looking at Ginny's back yard through his binoculars. He rubs his still sore neck and turns his head to one side popping the vertebrae. The lights are on poolside, but no one is in view.

RJ finishes his drink with a pain killer pill, pops his neck once again, picks up the rifle that is leaning against the wall, braces the bipod on the balcony railing, aims the rifle at a round vase on Ginny's patio and pulls the trigger. Click. The gun is not loaded. He wraps the gun in a blanket and hastily leaves his apartment making sure no one is in the hallway. He takes the stairs to the parking garage, being careful not to be seen. He puts the blanket wrapped rifle in the trunk, checks his watch and drives to the Everglades where he turns off onto the same road where he went target practicing. He stops the car, pops the trunk lid, takes the rifle out along with a spade and digs a hole that is a little larger than the rifle. RJ covers the new pit with brush, puts the rifle and spade back into the trunk, and drives off. He drives into the condo-parking garage, pulls into his parking place, and checks his watch. Perfect.

Halloween mid-afternoon. RJ is in the local super market preparing for the siege. He is buying "groceries": a bottle of whiskey, and a bag of ice. He then returns to his apartment and makes himself a large bourbon on the rocks. He walks out on the terrace with the drink and watches the caterers setting up for the party across the water.

Shortly after sunset the party guests begin to arrive. A band dressed as pirates begins playing. Costumed waiters and bartenders are at work.

A Headless Horseman arrives carrying a papier-mâché head. A multi-headed Hydra arrives with a multi-snaked Medusa. The snakes move with every step she takes. A husband and wife arrive as Goebbels and Goering. He is tall and heavyset. She's short and wiry.

Rasputin appears with a young, blond, rosy-cheeked Romanov prince, right out of Eisenstein's film Ivan the Terrible.

A man in a huge white wig, silk knickers, and an enormous walking stick with a death's head on the end of it has everyone puzzled as to who he is supposed to be. The Marquis de Sade? Whenever he reveals who he is his audience breaks into gales of laughter.

Harry appears as Captain Ahab. He has a terrible peg leg that wouldn't fool a blind man.

Another couple has costumed themselves as Baby Jane as in What-ever Happened to ... and Norman Bates' mother.

After all or most of the guests have arrived Ginny makes her entrance. Wig, cigarette holder, and garish makeup: outrageous screen star Tallulah Bankhead no doubt. She says something to some of the guests. Probably, thinks RJ reading her lips, one of Bankhead's now famous lines: "I'm pure as the driven slush."

One of the guests is saying something to Ginny that gets a big laugh. Ginny offers a Bankhead retort. RJ once again mouths the appropriate line. "Good evening, Miss Bankhead, sir."

RJ puts down the field glasses and goes to the kitchen where he makes himself another drink. The bottle of bourbon he bought earlier in the day is now considerably reduced. On the way back to the balcony with his refreshed drink, RJ picks up the rifle off the couch. He puts down his drink and loads the rifle. He scans the party through the night scope looking for Ginny. He stops on a large man with a mustache and a prop axe. The axe looks like something a comic Norseman would carry.

There is commotion from the side of the house. Two huge, burly men dressed in Mongolian outfits enter carrying a large golden platter. On top of the platter brandishing a large, curved scimitar stands Genghis Kahn: Dorsey has arrived; a tempting target.

Next he pans to Tallulah. Only this time she looks somewhat different, younger. RJ lowers the rifle and looks across to the party with a naked eye: two Tallulah's. What the hell is going on? Back to the rifle and the scope.

One of the Tallulah's is on the bandstand in front of the microphone saying something. Whatever she is saying, the crowd thinks it is hysterical. The other Tallulah climbs onto the stage, waves, and curtseys to the crowd, getting a big laugh. Number Two then leaves the stage and disappears into the crowd. To the accompaniment of the band Tallulah Number One walks to the microphone and begins singing.

"There's something in the air you can sense, elusive, and unbearably intense. The stars are hanging there in bright suspense, as they prepare to light immense events."

From off -stage Tallulah Number Two now reappears carrying a hand mike and begins singing a brilliant imitation of Number One as she joins her on the stage.

'Twas such a night as this, when Judy Garland swore: I just adore him, how can I ignore the boy next door?"

And then Number Two continues the song.

"On such a night did Gershwin write his rhapsody. On such a set did young Jeanette sing Lover Come Back To Me."

The phone rings in RJ's living room. He tries to ignore it, but it is incessant. Eventually he gives up and answers it.

"Hello?"

"Happy Halloween, old stain."

"Oh, it's you."

"And thrilled to hear from me I can tell. Did I wake you? I thought I saw you on your balcony a moment ago."

"You did. I'm awake. What's up?"

RJ walks with the phone out to the veranda.

"Listen, I've just had an idea concerning your little project that I'd like to discuss with you."

"Great. I'll be right over. Oh wait, I don't have a costume. How about lunch tomorrow instead?"

"Better yet, here, later tonight. At your ex's manse."

"Gee, Harry, what a great idea. We can have a little chat. The three of us. Just like old times."

"Listen up. The party is still in its infancy and the "hostess with the mostest" has already exceeded her limit of the powdery white stuff by at least half. Not to mention several gallons of Champagne. It's only a matter of time before she will be out like the proverbial light. The guests will have toddled off to bed and the caterers will have called it a night."

"This is all very interesting, Harry, but…"

"There is something here you must see. I'll call you when the time is right and the coast is clear."

"Who writes your stuff?"

But Harry has already hung up.

RJ returns to his roost. He takes a big slug of the bourbon and picks up the rifle. Trouble. The booze is starting to have an effect: big time double vision.

The Two Tallulah's are finishing their duet.

"On such a night as this did Robert Taylor sigh, as Garbo gave a little cough and wandered off to die. Lately I find I'm disinclined to reminisce, except perhaps on such a night as this."

The song ends. A huge round of applause. The Two Tallulah's take bows, hug each other, throw kisses, and generally camp it up.

The band starts another, much slower, tune that gradually slows down even more as if the phonograph needed to be cranked. The visual action has also shifted into slow motion.

As RJ views the scene through the night scope Tallulah Number One leaves the stage and takes a large drink of Champagne. She laughs and points directly into the lens at RJ.

RJ lowers the rifle and rubs his eyes. When he puts it back up he has difficulty finding Number One. There she is feeding a canapé to the Medusa and then pointing the finger once again at RJ. It's now or never. He has a clear shot and his vision has cleared.

He fires. Bango! The noise is deafening and there is an echo effect. Strange. What the hell's going on? He had a clear shot. How could he have missed?

Ginny has a puzzled look on her face. She looks right into the scope and then laughs and points again at RJ. The other guests also look up and laugh and point.

RJ fires blindly this time hitting a man in the back.

RJ fires again this time hitting one of Hydra's heads that shatters into a hundred pieces.

Genghis Kahn stands defiantly, arms akimbo, glaring in RJ's direction. RJ fires hitting him square in the chest. Dorsey can't believe he has been hit.

RJ is now in a panic. Where the hell is Ginny? There she is entering the house. As she opens the door she turns and looks right at RJ and shakes her head in disgust. Then she's gone.

"What's that sound? An intermittent noise way off somewhere."

RJ has fallen asleep with the rifle across his lap. He snaps awake and in the process falls over backwards; chair, rifle, glass, et al. He hits his head on the floor.

The glass, which is mostly water by this time, spills on his chest and the gun falls to the floor. Fortunately it doesn't go off.

The sound he was hearing is his phone and it is still ringing. RJ starts to move back into the living room, rubbing the back of his head, and runs right into the sliding glass door with his forehead. It almost knocks him out. Somehow he makes it to the phone.

"Hello?"

"Now. Right now. Come over. All the guests have left. The timing is perfect. She won't wake until around Thanksgiving."

"Harry, are you sure this is a good ... Harry?"

Harry has hung up. RJ still nursing his injuries hobbles to the front door. He remembers something and returns to the balcony. He rights the chair and picks up the rifle and the glass. On his way out he drops the rifle on the couch in the living room and the glass in the kitchen.

A few moments later he arrives at Ginny's. Harry is standing in the open front door. He has gotten rid of his peg leg and false whiskers. RJ parks his car and approaches the front door with some trepidation.

Harry sniffs.

"Bourbon? You don't look so good."

"Thank you, Harry, for pointing out my shortcomings once again."

Harry tries to touch the bump on RJ's head.

"Don't…"

They enter the foyer. RJ stops and looks at an illuminated painting. It appears to be a sketch of a man's head, but as you get closer it is also the skyline of a city.

"I like that painting. It's unique."

"Yes, I like it too. I gave it to Ginny for a wedding present. Always thought I might get it back one day. Fat chance."

"You never know. That's a nasty looking bump. You want some ice?"

"I'm fine. No big deal. Hit it on a door."

"Hmm."

They move into the living room that contains remnants of the party: glasses, dirty ashtrays, decorations, etc. And a sugar bowl half filled with a white powdery substance, some of which is spilled on the glass topped coffee table. Harry fills his glass with Champagne from an ice bucket.

"Champagne?"

RJ shakes his head no.

"Vintage. You won't get this every day."

"All right. Why not? Since herself is paying."

"That's the spirit."

"Spirit? I got it."

RJ takes the wine, sips and looks around the room.

"Nice place. Where's the mistress of the manor?"

"Out for the evening. Literally. Bring your glass I want to show you something."

RJ follows Harry into another room. The Champagne is not helping RJ. He's beginning to feel worse and is a little wobbly.

They enter the sunken study and there it is: an entire wall of pictures of Callie over the period of her short life: some portraits by professional photographers, some snap shots with Ginny and Chase, grandparents, birthday parties. RJ peruses the display stopping at one photo of Callie and her Raggedy Ann doll. RJ's mind is starting to play tricks on him. He thinks he sees Callie walking near the swimming pool. She is carrying her Raggedy Ann and talking to it.

"I gave her that doll on her second birthday. It was her favorite. She wouldn't go anywhere without it."

RJ is having a hard time staying in control of his emotions. He is also getting light headed and the double vision has returned. Callie is wandering precariously close to the edge of the pool.

"Was I right?"

"Huh? About what?"

Harry indicates the wall of pictures.

Callie is reprimanding her doll about something. She wags her finger at Raggedy Ann and drops her, accidentally, into the pool. RJ touches the bump on his head.

"Oh, yeah, the pictures. Absolutely. Thank you. You know, I'm not feeling so good. I think I'd better sit down."

They return to the living room where RJ falls into a large overstuffed leather chair.

"You were going to do it tonight weren't you?"

"How'd you know that?"

"I read you like a cheap novel. Don't ever play poker. So what happened? What stopped you?"

"I don't know. Jack from Kentucky played a large part."

"And, you know … bad omens. Or maybe just a case of no guts. Is it getting hot in here?"

"I'll open a window."

"But he doesn't move."

"I'm rather disappointed in you, old stain."

"What? Hey, what's with that "old stain" shit anyway"?

"You'd managed to convince me you had the strength of your convictions."

"You know, Harry, I've been thinking about that. I've tried very hard and I just can't remember ever telling you that I wanted to kill Ginny."

Harry looks at RJ a smile slowing appearing on his face.

"I believe you're correct, RJ, I can't remember you're saying it either. But, it seemed like such a good idea where ever it came from."

RJ's head is bobbing uncontrollably. He looks puzzled. He is having trouble following what Harry is saying, so he moves on to something else.

"Sometimes you have to get hit over the head to get the point. Fell over the goddamn gun. Could have shot myself. Too many Tallulahs."

One little, two little, three little Tallulahs … Callie in the swimming pool-ah. "Where's the bathroom?"

RJ looks at Harry and as he does Harry's head elongates. He is grinning. The effect is grotesque. RJ tries to set down his glass and it falls to the carpet.

"Howd' ju' do that?"

RJ tries to get out of the chair, but with no success.

"One little, two little … that's what she was … too little … too little to die."

With supreme effort RJ lurches to his feet and staggers outside to the swimming pool area.

RJ stares into the water. He sees the Raggedy Ann doll floating in the water. Callie walks to the edge of the pool, bends down and tries to reach her doll.

"No!!!"

Callie reaches even further for her doll and falls into the water.

"No, no, no!"

RJ lunges toward the living room and here on the landing still in her Tallulah outfit stands a very sober Ginny.

"Oh, shit…"

RJ tries desperately to focus. It looks like Ginny, all right, but somehow different. RJ manages to shake his head and clear his vision for one very short moment.

"Chase? You're … you're the…"

RJ falls face down on the stairs coming to rest just below Chase's feet. He rolls over and looks, from his upside down perspective, at Harry and Chase whose faces are oddly distorted. Harry has his arm around Chase. He spins Chase around, dips him over backwards, and kisses him on the mouth.

As he is losing consciousness, from far, far, away RJ hears a voice. Chase bends down very close to his face.

"Bye, bye, step-daddy, dearest."

"Ta ta for now, old stain. It's been fun."

RJ is wading in a swamp. The bottom is thick, boot sucking mud. It's very tough going. He isn't making much headway. He comes to a fallen tree and sits on it.

He takes off his boots and discovers a number of leeches on his feet and ankles. He tries to pull them off, but can't. They are too slippery and firmly entrenched. Suddenly there is a horrible smell in the air. RJ makes a grotesque face and covers his mouth and nose with his hand.

"Try a little bit more. I think he's coming around."

"What's goin' on?"

RJ looks up and sees a man in his mid to late fifties: a little bald and a little paunchy. A cop. L.C.BECK according to his ID badge.

"How ya' doin'? You okay?"

"Fine. Maybe not."

"You want some water? Give him some water."

RJ sips some water and coughs.

"Fine. I'm fine. Beck? What are you…?"

"Yeah, you look fine. Sorta'. Can you stand?"

"I don't know. I think so. Maybe."

He gets up with Beck's help.

"Good. Let's go outside."

They walk through the French doors out to the swimming pool where there is a whole crime scene; cop, police photographers and forensic specialists, etc. A man with a camera is taking pictures of the swimming pool. RJ and Beck walk to the edge of the pool. There near the bottom lies Ginny. At least we think its Ginny. RJ is beginning to suspect it might be smart to play dumb.

"Traffic copter spotted her from the air. Called us."

RJ and Beck watch the scene unfolding.

"They don't float."

"What?"

"Dead bodies. People think they float on the surface."

"They don't. Not until after they've been in the water for quite a while. Gas forms and they rise to the surface. Like a balloon."

As they watch a cop with a long pole fishes the body to the surface. It is Ginny. Beck takes out a pocket notebook.

"You know her?"

"My ex-wife."

"The one I met?"

"You met? Where?"

"Here when you daughter died. I interviewed her."

"That was you?"

"Yeah."

RJ stares at the body. "What happened?"

"I thought you might be able to tell me."

"I have no idea."

"Looks like she had a party. Had a little too much to drink, maybe some toot. We found a sugar bowl half full of cocaine in the living room. Maybe after everybody left she wandered out here, tripped, fell, hit her head, tumbled into the pool, and drowned. See what the coroner says. Sound feasible?"

"I guess so. I really don't have any idea."

"Or somebody killed her."

RJ keeps his mouth shut.

"One thing puzzles me: what are you doing here?" "According to a neighbor, it was a masquerade party and you don't seem to be in a costume."

"I wasn't at the party. I came over later. Am I a suspect?"

"A suspect of what? I just said it looks like an accident. Relax."

"Well, then I'm going to leave."

"Come on. Help me out with a couple a things. I'd like to wrap this thing up. I got a full plate this week."

"Can you make it fast? I'd really like to lie down."

"Sure. Just tell me, why did you come over here after the party?"

"A mutual friend of hers and mine, who was a guest at the party, called and asks me to come over for a nightcap … a glass of Champagne. Had something he wanted to show me. Said Ginny was asleep."

"What did he want to show you?"

"The shrine … the pictures of my daughter … in the study. I hadn't seen most of them."

"So, you had a drink, looked at the pictures and then what?"

"I don't know. I'd had a lot to drink earlier. I guess I just passed out."

"And your pal left you here for the ex-wife to find? Some pal."

"Yeah, I'll have to ask him about that next time I see him."

"What happened to your head? That's some bump."

"I guess I must have hit it on the floor when I passed out."

"If I were you I think I might consider going on the wagon."

"Not a bad idea."

"One more thing: any next of kin we should contact."

"She has a son. Chase. Chasin. I don't know where he lives, but I don't think it's here. You can probably reach him at the Pompano Beach Country Club. He works there."

"What's his last name?"

"Sanborn."

"This is her son, not yours?"

"That's right. Can I go now?"

"Absolutely. And thanks for your help. I appreciate it."

RJ starts to head for the living room and the front door.

"Oh, here, take my card. Call me if you think of anything."

"Just like on TV. I think I've got one. From before."

"Right. Take another one just in case."

"Like what?"

"Who knows?"

RJ starts to leave again. Beck is looking over his notes.

"Oh, say … Mr. McCaw… this Harry guy … what's his last name?"

"MacDivitt. Two t's."

"Where can I reach him?"

"He has a house on Sunsuit Boulevard. Right off..."

"Yeah, I know where it is. Only a block long. Funny name. Get some sleep. You look lousy."

"Thank you, I will."

Later RJ walks out of his bathroom wearing a robe and drying his hair with a towel. He looks somewhat better, but tired. As he crosses to the kitchen the doorbell rings. RJ opens the front door. Detective Beck stands there smiling.

"One Man's Family."

"What?"

"One Man's Family; the old radio show. It was sponsored by Chase and Sanborn ... the coffee company. Your kid's Chasin Sanborn ... Chase and Sanborn. You mean to tell me you never thought of that before?"

"I don't think so. And he's not my kid. Stepson. Former stepson. Ex-stepson ... whatever."

"Oh, yeah, right. Afraid my memory is not what it used to be. Maybe I got ... what's the name of that disease when you can't remember anything?"

"You're a regular comedian. Dementia."

"Yeah, maybe that's my problem."

"I don't think so."

"What's that?"

"I think it's a ruse. There's nothing wrong with your memory. You're kinda' the Dixie Sergeant Columbo aren't you? Where's your trench coat?"

"You know you'd be surprised how much of the time it works."

"I'll bet. I just made some fresh coffee. You want some?"

"Oh, yeah, that would be great."

They both move to the kitchen. On the way Beck notices the torn picture that Callie drew for RJ. The one Ginny tried to destroy. The pieces are now pasted together and framed. Beck sits at the counter on a bar stool while RJ pours.

"Milk or sugar?"

"Both, if you got it."

RJ does the honors and stands across from Beck after he serves the coffee. Beck sips.

"Oh, that's good. Chase and Sanborn?"

"Folger's. So, Lieutenant, what's up?"

But Beck has moved into the living room where the rifle is still lying on the couch.

"Hey, what's this?"

RJ follows and sees the gun just as Beck puts down his coffee cup and picks it up.

"I haven't seen one of these in a long time."

Beck opens the breech.

"And loaded, too. You keep a loaded gun with the safety off just lying around your apartment? Good thing you don't have any kids. Oh, I…"

"Anymore."

"Yeah, right. Sorry."

"Don't worry about it. Water over the bridge, as my ex-wife used to say."

"Water over the bridge? That one of those, ah…"

"Malaprops."

"Yeah, Malaprops. So, what's with the gun?"

"I was thinking of going hunting."

"Really? What were you thinking of going hunting for?"

"I don't know, varmints, maybe."

Beck unloads the gun and takes it out to the balcony. RJ follows.

"Varmints? What a funny idea. Buy an expensive rifle to hunt rats. Why not just a twenty-two? Hey, you can see your ex's place from here."

Beck raises the rifle and aims at the pool. There are still cops there.

"Whoa, that was a dumb idea. Might get shot by one of my own men. Think I was a sniper or somethin'."

Beck smiles and looks at RJ as if the sniper idea just occurred to him.

"Are you in her will, by any chance?"

"Ha! I don't think so. We had a very nasty divorce."

"Just a thought. So, you wouldn't stand to benefit from her death?"

"Not in the least. The only thing she has that I would want is a picture that hangs in her front hallway. I gave it to her for a wedding present."

"The picture of the guy's head that's really a skyline?"

"Yes. That and a photo of Callie holding a Raggedy Ann doll. Other than that … nothing."

"I got it."

"Look, I'm fading like a two-dollar sport shirt…"

"Oh, right, sorry. I get to thinking, you know, and … well, I'll be going. I appreciate your time."

RJ and Beck move to the front door.

"I keep askin' myself why is it that you're practically livin' in her backyard?"

"My being here is just a coincidence. A friend knew of this place and got it for me very reasonably. That's all there is to it. Look, Detective, I really am exhausted."

"Oh, yeah, right. Sorry. Just one more thing; you have any idea why she might want to kill herself?"

"Kill herself? What makes you think that?"

"Just a thought. Sometimes it's hard to tell if a drowning victim's done himself or herself in or they've

135

been murdered. No cuts or bruises in one case. No suicide note in another. Very tough."

"Are you saying we may never know for sure?"

"Quite possibly. The thing I was wondering … she walks out of the house and drops into the pool … wouldn't she have thought it a little odd that her ex-husband was right there…"

She might not have seen me. She could have come down the outside second floor stairway directly to the pool bypassing the first floor altogether.

"That's very good. Very well thought out. You'd be a good detective. Well, I'll be on my way. Thanks for the coffee. Chase 'n Sanborn. Funny. I'll give you a call after the autopsy. Let you know what we find."

"Thank you, I'd appreciate that."

"Happy hunting. Oh, don't leave town without checking with me first."

"I thought you said I wasn't a suspect."

"That was before I saw the gun. We find a bullet in your ex, needless to say, changes everything."

Beck leaves. RJ gets some more coffee and walks to the balcony overlooking the crime scene. He stares into the water of the pool.

RJ lies down but finds that he is wide-awake. He mind goes back to the first time he saw Ginny. It was the senior class prom party at the Joliet, Illinois Country Club. A band plays in one corner of the large second story ballroom. Graduating seniors are dancing to a 1950's song. Above the din of the band and the kids we hear a wolf whistle. Take it off! Another voice answers, Take it all off!

The band continues to play, but the dancers all head for the second story balcony that is on the same level as the high diving board. One of the young men returns to the ballroom where he says something to the leader of the band.

Ginny is doing a striptease on the high diving board to the encouragement of twenty or more of her fellow classmates. She has removed her ball gown and is stepping out of her crinoline slip that she balls up and throws toward the crowd poolside. The slip lands on the head on inebriated student who is more intent on trying to light a cigarette then paying attention to the events unfolding on the diving board. The band is now blaring the song The Stripper.

RJ is entranced. Right in front of him is the most beautiful girl he has ever seen. Another young man RJ's age looks on disapprovingly and says to RJ, "That girl is trouble. Real big trouble. I heard she once fucked the entire varsity football team"

She is now dressed in only underpants and bra. She makes her approach to the end of the board, springs once and is air borne. RJ is aware that she has executed a perfect dive; cutting through the surface of the water without creating so much as a ripple. She is under the water for a very long time. When she finally surfaces there is a big smile on her face.

RJ has given up on trying to sleep and is still standing on the balcony with his coffee. His eyes are misting over.

Poolside at Ginny's is much the same, except there are no longer any police; just yellow plastic cordons around the swimming pool itself. RJ re-enters the condo and closes the drapes.

When RJ arrived at work the next day, hung over from lack of sleep, Frankie was all a twitter.

"You see this?"

He was holding a copy of the Miami Herald. PROMINENT ATTORNEY SLAIN IN GULF.

Scanning the article Frankie summarizes and reads what he considers pertinent parts. "According to the story, an anonymous caller had told the police they would find André's body attached to the leg of an abandoned offshore drilling rig seven miles out of Grand Isle, Louisiana. There was only one rig in that area. Sure enough, after a minimal amount of searching by police divers, there he was. His hands were tied behind him and a plastic bag was taped over his head. Sharks had already been working on him.

Police were quoted as saying they had no idea who killed him. No clues whatsoever. According to the article, when last seen he was in his office in Atlanta the site of his former law firm. Armed with a search warrant, the police entered the office and found it in complete disarray. Files were thrown all over the place. Legal documents had been burned in a wastebasket on the balcony.

In addition, a security guard was found strangled in the under-ground parking lot. Police refused to speculate on whether or not the two killings were related."

Frankie hands the paper to RJ who quickly scans the piece looking for any mention of Angeline or Lobo. Nothing.

RJ gets her home phone number from André's file in Frankie's office. A telephone company recorded message says that the service had been discontinued. No forwarding number.

Momentarily he thinks, Just as well. The timing was all wrong. He didn't the need the distraction. But he couldn't get her out of his mind. He was sure eventually she would call. It would just be a matter of time.

On the weekend RJ, top down on his car, exits the highway turning eventually on to Sunset Boulevard. RJ parks his car in front of Harry's house. A middle-aged, balding, man in a Hawaiian shirt and Bermuda shorts is watering the flowers in the front with a garden hose. RJ approaches him.

"'Morning."

The Man frowns at RJ.

"I'm looking for Mr. MacDivitt. Is he in?"

"You and every bill collector in town. He owe you money?"

"Not a dime."

"Wish I could say the same."

"Is it a lot? What he owes you?"

"Let's see, there's the back rent. That's in the neighborhood of ten grand. Then there's the Corvette he leased in my name. Police found it stripped in a parking lot near the Miami airport. The huge bills at the country club that the club is holding me responsible for just because I got him a guest membership. Yeah, I'd say it was a lot."

"Right. I'd say so too. I'm very sorry. Well, thanks for your help. Say, one more thing: have the police been around here?"

"A couple of times. They want to ask him about some babe they found in a swimming pool somewhere."

"I see. Well, thanks again."

RJ walks back to his car leaving the Man with his watering.

A cemetery much like all cemeteries. RJ stands watching from a short distance away. Ginny is being buried. Some of the same people who were at the Halloween party are there along with Ginny's mother Helene and stepfather Henry. Dorsey is being rolled in a wheelchair by a uniformed chauffeur. It is evident he has had a stroke or a heart attack. The minister is finishing speaking, "Someone once wrote "the tears of yesterday have turned to rain." Dear Virginia, rest in peace."

RJ is unaware of someone walking up behind him.

"I thought you might be here."

RJ turns to find the detective.

"Detective Beck. Fancy meeting you here."

They watch the mourners arriving.

"I mentioned your name to your ex-mother-in-law the other day."

"Oh?"

"Oh?" That's it? You're not curious about what she said?

They watch the graveside service in silence.

"Nuttin'"

"Nuttin'?"

"That's what she had to say. Nothing. Guess you two weren't real close."

"You might say that. But we aren't enemies either. She knows that I hold her daughter responsible for Callie's death."

"She didn't mention that. Then again why would she? Her husband … her new husband … told me when she was out of the room, that you were a good father to your daughter."

"He did? He said that? What' da' ya' know Joe? So, tell me, did you find a bullet?"

"No. She hadn't been shot and you're no longer a suspect."

"I wasn't sure I was. However, I'm relieved. I've heard tell of innocent people spending a lot of time in jail."

"Happens. Anyway, the coroner's report came in and it was a little peculiar, but he's ruled it was an accident."

"What was the peculiar part?"

"You remember we found this sugar bowl half full of cocaine? The coroner couldn't find any evidence of drugs of any kind in her system. Booze yeah, but no drugs."

"Is that right?"

"So, anyway, what I wanted to ask you … how do you feel about your ex-wife drowning in the same swimming pool as you daughter?"

"Feel? I don't feel anything at all. Coincidence. A very unfortunate coincidence, that's all."

"I thought that's what you might say. But, being a cop we're taught to be very leery of coincidence. So, how did you react when your daughter died?"

"I'll tell you, Beck … say what's your first name, anyway?"

"I'll never tell."

"Can't be that bad. Leo? Larry? Lance?"

Beck stonewalls.

"Speaking of which what's your full first and second names?"

"First name is RJ. That's it. No second name."

"RJ? Just RJ? Weird. So, anyway back to how you felt when your daughter died. Other than remorse, of course."

"RJ Thinks for a minute pondering the possible consequences of his answer."

"Angry. Very, very angry."

"Angry enough to shoot her with a varmint rifle?"

Now it's RJ's turn to stonewall.

"That day down at the boat yard where you work … you were pretty upset. Almost out of control…"

RJ concludes very quickly that the best answer to this is no answer at all.

"Then again, no man in his right mind would try to get away with killing his ex-wife when she lives practically next door, would he? And you're not crazy are you?"

RJ once again chooses the course of no comment.

"Did you talk to Harry MacDivitt?"

"Couldn't find him. Or the son."

"Did you try the club?"

"Didn't come back to work after his mother died. Both he and this MacDivitt guy have disappeared off the face of the planet. I was surprised to find out who owns the condo you live in."

"Who does?"

"The kid ... Chasin. You didn't know that? Come on."

"I had no idea. I wouldn't have lived there if I'd known. I send a check to the building board of directors each month and I just assumed they passed it on to the owner."

"Another of those weird coincidences. See what I mean?"

"I'm beginning to. So, now what?"

"Unless something turns up down the road ... death by accidental drowning. Finito. Case closed."

"One thing that puzzles me, if Harry had so much of his own money why would he need Ginny's."

"You're talking about the rubbers through the mail."

"Right."

"Great story and it really did happen only not to Mr. MacDivitt. I read about this in the paper some time ago. The guy lives in Chicago. Likes the money, but is embarrassed about how he made it."

"You're a veritable encyclopedia of information."

"I come about it naturally. My mother was a history teacher."

The burial accumulation is breaking up. As the people file back to their cars Dorsey looks in RJ's direction. His face distorts and he raises his hand, index finger extended in the form of a gun and points it at RJ.

"A very angry man, eh?"

"You don't know the half of it. Matter of fact, neither do I. Well I gotta' go'. Maybe when I get ready to retire I'll see you about buyin' a fishin' boat."

"Sure, why not. Give you a deal. You know, a friend of the family. You know where to find me."

"Take care of yourself."

"Yeah, you too."

Beck crosses the street to his car and leaves. RJ watches the last of the funeral procession depart. He walks toward the gravesite where two workers are starting to fill the hole with earth. The two workers ignore him and go about their business. After a moment RJ takes some of the flowers off Ginny's grave and places them on Callie's. He stands there awhile between the two graves.

"So, Ginny, what's the story?"

"We'll probably never know, will we?"

Startled, RJ turns to the voice. It's Ginny's mother Helene. She holds a large package.

"No, I guess not."

"Chase called this morning to tell me he wouldn't be here. I just don't understand that boy."

"Did he say why or where he was?"

"No. He said he thought it was better I didn't know."

"Very cryptic."

She hands the package to RJ.

"I thought you might like to have these. It's the painting you gave her as a wedding present and the photograph of Callie with Raggedy Ann."

RJ takes the package.

"Thank you."

Helene takes an envelope out of her purse and hands it to RJ.

"And this is from me. It's a check."

"I don't understand. Is this some kind of blood money? I don't want this."

"Don't be... (Catches herself) It never should have ended this way. The whole thing has been so ... I don't know. What's the word I want?"

"Tragic?"

"Too theatrical. Sad, I think."

She holds out the check envelope again.

"RJ, please, take it. Try to find some happiness for yourself. I know this is only a token, but it might help. Ease the pain, maybe even if it's only temporary."

Reluctantly RJ takes the envelope. Helene kisses him on the cheek and starts to walk back toward her car where her husband Henry is waiting.

"And you, Helena. How will you deal with all of this?"

Helena just smiles; a sad, terribly lonely smile.

"If you ever hear from Chase, again, tell him ... tell him..."

Helene has stopped and looks at RJ.

"Tell him what?"

RJ has no reply.

"I don't know."

"Right. Good-bye, RJ."

She continues toward her car.

A gorgeous day off the coast of Miami. Not just a pretty day, a glorious day. Retired Lieutenant L. C. Beck is at the helm of the Baracuta. RJ loosens a line and adjusts the foresail.

"RJ calls to Beck, "Ease her off a bit."

144

Beck makes the adjustment.

"That's it. Hold her there."

RJ comes aft and sits near Beck.

Beck smiles and says, "Man, I love this boat."

"Me too."

"Tell me somethin' what are those things on the stern for?"

"The dinghy. They're called dingy davits. They're for hauling the dingy out of the water when maybe you're taking a long trip and don't want to drag it behind the boat. Slows it down. Might come loose and you lose it."

"Got it. Funny name. Dingy Davits. Sounds like the name of a TV comedy character. Is it still for sale?"

"Not at the moment. I tried to buy it, but by the time I got around to making an offer Ray had a change of heart."

"Rather than a change of mind?"

"Right. I think the boat was somehow all tied up with his wife. Maybe he couldn't bear the idea of selling it. Loyalty, maybe. Who knows?"

"Understandable."

"We had it at the yard for quite some time. Had a couple of low-ball offers that Ray rejected out of hand. Then he started taking it out once in a while. Just to check it out he said. Make sure everything was ship shape. Finally he took it off the market. When I asked him why he said that he had discovered that it was, as he called it, "a pussy magnet.""

"That's funny. Boy, is this a great day?"

"Perfect. Can't wait to leave."

"Leave? Are you nuts! To go where? This is paradise."

"For you, yeah. For me, I need a break. I've got some vacation time coming."

"Where you gonna' go? The Caribbean, I'll bet."

"Maybe. Ray and his fiancé are going to Italy for a month. Visit her family. He says I can use the boat. Go anywhere I want to. Want to join me?"

"I can't. Too much family stuff. Kid's getting married."

"Then again I'm also thinking about Spain, maybe. Pamplona. Run with the bulls."

"You're crazy."

"I thought you already decided I wasn't."

"I've changed my mind."

"You may be right, Lamar. Ludwig? Lyndon? Wait, I got it: Leslie. Right? That's it isn't it? But what's your middle name? Let's see…"

"Give it up."

After a moment Beck says, "Look, if I tell you you gotta' promise you'll never tell a living soul."

"Promise."

"My mother wanted a girl. Before I was born she already had a girls' name picked out. When I turned up she kept the name."

RJ thinks for a moment.

"Elsie?"

"Right. After Elsie the Borden cow. You know Borden's is a dairy. Great ice cream. Don't forget your promise."

"Don't worry about it. My lips are sealed."

"To change the subject how are you coming with your search for McDivitt and the kid?"

"Oh, I gave that up long ago. The proverbial needle in a haystack. Besides, what was I going to do if I'd found them? You'd already said the case was closed."
"Accidental death."

"Right. Good decision."

Ray Arbuthnot and a rather frumpy, but fun looking middle-aged woman come up from the galley carrying a wine bucket, glasses and lunch. They seem crazy about each other.

"Who's for Champagne?"

A golf course in a tropical setting somewhere in the Caribbean. Dark, ominous, clouds overhead and very breezy. A foursome is just finishing putting out on the ninth green just as a heavy downpour arrives sending them scurrying for the clubhouse. A bartender is waiting is waiting with their drinks. They take their cocktails and walk to the edge of the veranda and watch the rain coming down.

The golfers' attention is drawn to the deck entry to see a young man carrying a stack of clean, white towels that he hands out to each man. The young man is Chase.

RJ is perched in a tree looking at the unfolding scene. He is holding a different, much more sophisticated rifle than the one he had earlier and wearing camouflage. He raises the gun and pans the four men stopping on Harry.

Part Two

Early in the 1970's.The Atlantic coast of France somewhere just south of Biarritz close to the Spanish border. A modern large glass and white washed building on a cliff with a spectacular view of the Atlantic. It is a three star restaurant with an enormous kitchen that is open to the dining room. Every table is occupied.

A very attractive middle-aged couple is having lunch. Jordan Christopher is tall with a full head of gray hair. He has a slight suntan. His wife, Dixie Lee, is the epitome of what happens to a woman in her sixties who has taken extreme care of herself. She has short blond hair, a practically line free face and bright blue eyes. A looker.

Jordan says, "Hilarious."

"What is?"

"What is what?"

"Who's on first?"

"Why am I having trouble following this conversation?"

"You're having trouble? It started with my saying I really liked this restaurant and then you said 'hilarious.'"

"Sorry."

After a slight pause while she takes a puzzled look at her husband she says, "So, what's the news you've been waiting to tell me newsman?"

My agent got a call from the W.W.N. yesterday. They're starting a new international cable news network to be based, for some reason, in Madrid. They're looking for an anchor for the evening edition and they want to know if I would be interested.

"What did you say?"

"I told him I'd think about it. Talk it over with you. I don't know. Be nice to be employed again. It's intriguing but, after what happened, I think this part of France is about as close as I ever want to get to Spain."

Jordan's eyes wander around the room and stop at the open kitchen where several cooks are preparing food.

"Jordan, are you all right? You look awfully pale all of a sudden. You don't think it's the mussels do you? Remember the last time…"

"I'm fine. I wonder if there is a name for deja vu when you actually remember what it was your mind thinks happened before."

"I believe it's called a good memory. Something I wish I had. What do you think you just remembered?"

"I saw someone I thought I knew, that's all."

Dixie turns around and looks around the room.

"Where?"

"Please, don't do that."

Starting to get genuinely concerned she says, "You're making me very nervous. What is going on?"

"Would you do something for me? Go to the ladies room. As you walk by the kitchen take a look at the tall man with the big handlebar mustache. And please, try very hard not to be obvious about it."

She is used to this kind of thing. She considers for a moment and then does as he asks. As she passes the food preparation area the mustachioed man in all white wearing a chef's hat is de-boning a large fish. As she passes by the open kitchen she catches the man's eye. At first he smiles, seeing only a pretty woman, but very quickly that smile changes to some form of recognition. He's seen her before, he thinks. And then he remembers. His eyes scan the dining room stopping as they meet Jordan's and then quickly he turns his attention back to the fish. Jordan has belatedly avoided the Chef's glance and is looking out the window next to his table.

The set of CBC News three years earlier.

Jordan, the prime time news anchor and "most watched man in America," is on the air. Part of Jordan's appeal lies in his looks. He typifies what we have come to believe a news anchor should look like with an authoritarian voice that can command attention and or sympathy.

"Good evening. We begin tonight's program with the President's trip next week to Spain for the International Peace Conference in Madrid, the largest meeting of world leaders ever. With a report on how preparations are or are not moving along, here is Paul Serrano in Madrid. Good evening, Paul, how are things shaping up?"

Outside a government building in Madrid. Correspondent Paul Serrano... A Spanish and English speaking man in his mid to late thirties.

"Well, Jordan, I suppose that depends on your perspective. If you own a hotel or a top restaurant they couldn't be better. They're booked solid and have been for at least two months. If you're in the security business it's another story. Rumors are already circulating about what ETA, the extremist arm of the Basque separatist movement, is planning. Everything from bombings of government buildings to kidnappings of politicians. They've done it before; they're capable of doing it again. The tension factor appears to rising each day. We'll just have to wait and see."

"Thank you, Paul. Tomorrow night marks the official beginning of the conference although any real business won't be conducted until Tuesday. Michael Bodkin reports on the opening night festivities. Michael."

In Madrid at the Plaza de Independencia. Michael Bodkin another correspondent. Much older and experienced than Serrano he gives the impression of having 'been there.'

"I'm standing in front of the Plaza de Independencia, arguably one of Madrid's most recognizable landmarks. It's where tomorrow night's parade will begin. All the official representatives of the conference will be in the procession in closed cars making for an all-out alert by Spain's security forces. And if that's not bad enough, a fireworks display, which is being touted as the world's largest and most spectacular, will be going off as they pass along the route. Hold on to your hats."

"Indeed. Thank you, Michael. We'll back with more of today's news after this."

That same day in the Miami offices of WHERE IN THE WORLD, INC. RJ now in his early fifties stands watching the news. He is trying to record it and is having trouble with the machine. The TV news broadcast continues in the background with a serial killer story.

"Carmella, can you come in here, please? And hurry."

Carmilla Espinosa, a Latina in her mid-thirties enters the office.

"I can't get this damn thing to work. You'd think after all these years I could figure it out but I can't. I want to make sure we get the new spot."

Carmella walks over to the TV with the remote control in her hand and in a few seconds 'Now Recording' comes up on the screen. She hands him back the remote and starts to leave. There are now commercials showing on the screen.

"Thank you. Don't ever quit. Wait a second. Stay here I want you to see this. Let me know what you think."

As one spot ends *Where in the World*'s commercial begins. RJ is the spokesman. He is standing on a remote palm tree strewn beach and is wearing white trousers and an outlandishly colorful short-sleeved shirt. No houses, boats or people.

"This is some people's idea of paradise. No cars, no television, no noise. Complete isolation from the rest of the world. Paradise. But it might get boring after a while. You might want to see the Super Bowl or the Oscar's. If you've often thought of changing your life for the better, but haven't a clue as to do it, we can help. Over the last ten years *Where In The World* has helped thousands of people find a newer, better way of life. It's not difficult and it does take a little time and effort, but if you could be living in your own personal paradise wouldn't it be worth it?"

A super appears on the screen with the name of the company, address, and telephone number. Another spot begins.

"So, what do you think?"

"Not bad. Only time will tell."

As Carmella is heading back to her office she turns and says, "Nice shirt."

The news is back on.

"In another story from Spain tonight word comes of still one more in a series of grisly murders of young homosexual men. Karl Lepinsky from Marbella."

Lepinsky is standing in front of a police crime scene in Marbella.

"Local police officials and the Guardia Civil are searching for any kind of clue that would lead them to whoever is killing these young gay men. Juan Moreno, a real estate salesman from Torremolinos, was found stuffed into a garbage bin early this morning in back of one of Marbella's most fashionable boutiques. This makes number ten and, unless they discover something soon, who knows where it will end. Jordan."

"Karl Lepinsky in Marbella. That's it for now. I'll be reporting Monday and all next week with the President in Madrid. Have a pleasant weekend."

Later that evening RJ enters the Star Bar and sits down next to Tom Drum, an old friend.

"Hey, RJ, what's the haps?"

"Just saw our new commercial on the news."

"Yeah, I just saw it. Nice shirt."

"Is it really that bad?"

"No, not really, or yes, depending on how you look at it."

Todd the bartender approaches.

"Mr. McCaw, how ya' doin'?"

"Thirsty."

"What'll it be? Hey, I saw your commercial a few minutes ago."

In unison RJ and Tom say, "Nice shirt!"

"How'd you know I was gonna' say that?"

"I wonder. Give me a light rum and club soda with a squeeze. Lotsa' ice."

To Drum, "So, who's it gonna' be, the Dolphin's or the Bears?"

"I don't know. The Bears, I'm afraid, but anyway I can't go."

"What? Why not? I thought we had a plan."

The bartender brings RJ'S drink. Another male customer enters the bar and takes a seat a dozen or so places from RJ and Drum.

"Hold onto your shorts. You can have both tickets."

Drum hands them over to RJ.

"I just can't go and I don't want to talk about it."

"Let me guess…"

"Are you my friend? Because, if you are, don't guess."

"What's the word I'm looking for…? Oh, yeah, "co" something. Co-depend …"

"Careful. (He slugs his drink.) I gotta' go."

Drum leaves some money on the bar.

"I'll take the Dolphins and ten."

"Do I really look that stupid?"

"Yeah. Ever since the "shirt.""

Drum leaves. RJ takes a big slug of his drink. He looks at the MIAMI HERALD that has been left on the bar. He glances at it but nothing catches his eye. He finishes his drink.

"Un otra?"

"What?"

"Un otra. Another in Spanish."

"I didn't know you spoke Spanish."

"I don't, but I got a new girlfriend and…."

"She does."

"You got it. Anyway, you want un otra?"

"Yeah, I got an hour and a half before the game. But, maybe a beer. I don't want to get loaded."

"Bud?"

"Spare me."

From the only other customer sitting at the bar comes, "How about a Guinness?"

RJ freezes. The voice is from the man who came in moments ago. He is in his middle to late sixties. He has a tan, white hair tied in a ponytail, and he is wearing a white suit. A Panama hat sits on a bar stool next to him. He is also wearing expensive sunglasses.

This guys a friend of yours?

"Not even remotely."

"Cause' if you want…"

"Be a good little boy and bring us a pair of Guinness."

"Draught."

"It's all right, Todd. Nothing to worry about. So, Harry, what brings you out from under your rock?"

"Still the funny one, eh, RJ."

"That's me the life of the party. Or is it the fall guy of the party? How would you characterize me, Harry?"

"Clever. Very clever. And it's Neville now, by the way."

"Neville? You don't say. Why am I not surprised? You change names like some guys change socks. And what little con game brings you back to Florida? No, wait, I don't want to know."

Harry moves closer to RJ.

"May I?"

RJ doesn't respond. He just stares at Harry.

"What do you want … Harry?"

Ignoring the question, Harry says, "How are you, RJ? You look fit and prosperous."

"Well, I'm alive and not spending the rest of my life in jail, no thanks to you."

"May I have my check, please, Todd?"

He gets up and takes some money out of his wallet.

"I need your help, RJ."

Todd returns with the beers.

RJ laughs. "Sure. Glad to help. How'd you find me, Harry?"

"Telephone book."

"Yeah, right. Funny, I thought I had an unlisted number. What do you want?"

"Chase is missing and I want ... would like ... you to help me find him."

"I help you find the other half of the dynamic duo that tried to frame me for the murder of my ex-wife? What a great idea. Wrong guy, Harry. Definitely the wrong guy. But I'm curious, whatever gave you the idea I would want to help you?"

Harry notices that the bartender is watching them while polishing glasses.

"Do you suppose we could talk about this somewhere a little less public?"

As the sun is beginning to set RJ and Harry ... Neville... are walking along Ocean Avenue in South Beach. RJ is obviously irritated at Harry and, also, at himself for even listening to ... whatever his name is.

"C'mon, Harry, do you expect..."

"Neville, actually."

"Yeah, right. How soon I forget. Must be my age or ... or... You know what? For some time now I have not known what to believe with you. From now on I'm going to operate on the assumption that you're lying. And, as far as what to call you is concerned, should I be unfortunate enough to see you again, I'm going to stick with Harry. Neville sounds too goddamned ... what ... respectable maybe ... I don't know."

Harry takes a piece of paper out of his pocket. RJ keeps moving, picking up the pace.

"This is a letter to you from your son."

RJ stops and glares at Harry.

"I don't have a son, Harry. I had a daughter, but she's dead. I did have a stepson, for about an hour and a half, but no real son. And who would know that better than you his … whatever you guys call each other."

"I appreciate your restraint. I never have liked being called a fag. Who would? Call me the Queen of the fucking May, for all I care, if you'll just read this."

"I don't want to read it … whatever it is. The only thing I'd like to read about you is your obituary. I'm not Nick Carter Tracer of Lost Persons and I am not going to get suckered into another one of your wild-assed schemes. I'm going home now. I'd like to say it's been nice seeing you again, Harry, but, unlike yourself, I gave up lying for lent."

Later that evening at home RJ holds the letter in his hand. He is staring into the darkness. A Raggedy Ann doll sits in a prominent position in the room. A handsome woman dressed for bed walks into the room. It's Joanna Blair, RJ's girlfriend.

"I'm turning in. Are you coming?"

RJ doesn't respond.

"Are you okay?"

"What? Yeah, I'm fine."

"How many more times are you going to read that?"

"No more. I've had it. You've looked at this. What do you make of it?"

"I don't know … all that stuff about Chases' mother, your ex-wife … it does sound odd at the very least. Could you possibly be his father?"

"I'll spare you the lurid details, but if what he says his mother told him is true, then yes, I suppose I could."

"If it is true why would she tell her son about an affair with you years before you were married?"

"The sixty four dollar question. I have no idea. However, coming from Ginny, any explanation is possible. As I have said many, times Ginny had only a passing acquaintance with the truth. If there were two ways to tell a story... one was the truth and another version was more entertaining... you could bet your boots she'd take the later."

"Then I guess the thing is what, if anything, are you going to do about it?"

"All these years...I thought I was through with all this."

"What does ... what's his name, Harry, want you to do?"

"He wants me to go with him to Spain. Try and find his ... buddy. He says that because Chase speaks Spanish and is a golf pro that's the logical place for him to be. Although there are lotsa' golf courses, Harry says he has an idea where he will probably be. Although he has yet to divulge to me where that might be."

"And if you find him, then what?"

"I don't know. Talk to him. Find out who he is. Is he really my kid? Ask him about what really happened to his mother, I don't know. The whole thing's nuts."

"What makes you think he'll tell you?"

"Why write me this letter? What's the point? If he really is my son I'd like to know. Harry says he thinks he's in some sort of trouble. That he's been acting peculiarly. Maybe suicidal."

"And you believe him?"

"I don't know what to believe. He's lied to me before, but what if this time he's telling the truth. If I don't do anything to help this kid and something happens to him? Then what?"

"Then you've got some more guilt baggage to go along with the stuff you're already carrying about your daughter."

"Exactly. Get out the checkbook and go back to the shrink."

"So, what are you gonna' do?"

RJ just looks at her for a moment.

"When my daughter died something in me died too. I've tried to figure it out…it's a part of me that's missing. A fear of closeness, maybe. Afraid of being hurt again, I don't know. The shrink couldn't figure it out either. So I gave up on her."

"Don't be so hard on yourself. That's my job."

She has a slight, loving smile on her face.

"Yeah, right. So, maybe … in some strange way … if I can find Chase maybe I'll get it back… whatever it is. Does that make sense?"

Joanna sits on RJ's lap, puts her arms around him, and kisses him.

"All the sense in the world. Don't stay up too late."

RJ sits alone contemplating what to do. He looks around the room and his eyes settle on the Raggedy Ann doll and, as is usually the case, just looking at the doll can transport him into the past.

RJ and Callie who is three years old at this time are having a great day together. They are walking hand in hand along a sidewalk that parallels a beach. Callie is carrying her brand new Raggedy Ann doll that still has a sales tag on it. It is obvious that RJ adores his little girl. He has tried several times to remove the tag, but she wants to keep it on. She says it's Raggedy Ann's jewelry.

The next day RJ and Harry are hurrying to catch a plane. They are each carrying a suitcase and a smaller bag.

RJ says, "We have to make this flight. I can't tell you the favors I had to cash in to get these seats. Some big deal is going on in Madrid. Everybody and his brother are either on the way to Madrid or already there."

"Why Madrid anyway? Why not just get a connecting flight and go directly to Malaga and Marbella where all the golf courses are?"

"I want to see the people at the Federacion del Golf, or whatever it's called. I'm hoping they can help us. Maybe they have a list of all the golf pros in Spain. Might save us a lot of time. And they're in Madrid."

"Why not just call them?"

"I did. They said that kind of information was confidential. At least I think that's what the guy said. His English was almost as good as my Spanish."

They are approaching the gate and an airline representative is waving to them to hurry. They show their tickets, he takes the suitcases and points them in the direction of the coach section.

Harry whines, "We're riding in the tourist section? Steerage?"

"Look, we're lucky to get seats at all."

As they pass through the first class section RJ notices Jordan Christopher and his entourage. Jordan and an attractive woman are seated having a pre-flight glass of champagne. She is at least twenty years younger than Jordan and striking. Her name is Stacey Parker and she is a production assistant on the evening news. Two producers sit behind them. Stacey leans over and speaks softly to Jordan.

"I am so excited. My first time to Europe and I'm riding in first class, drinking a glass of champagne and sitting next to the world's sexiest man."

She knows exactly how to appeal to Jordan's massive ego.

"Wait till you see the hotel in Madrid. The Ritz is truly one of the great hotels of the world."

"I've heard it must be terribly expensive."

"Not something I'd think you'd have to worry about. I thought your father was loaded."

"Yes, but…"

"Just kidding. All expenses paid by the network of course. We do, however, have to be very discreet. The Spanish press is merciless. And I'll bet every paparazzi in Europe has descended on Madrid for the conference."

"I'll try to be good."

"Not too good, I trust."

They share a wicked little laugh, which gets a raised eyebrow from the producers behind them.

Meanwhile, Harry is smiling at a male steward.

Upon arriving at the Barajas airport in Madrid RJ and Harry are putting their things in a cab. Jordan and one of the producers are getting into a limo with a local producer. Stacey and the other New York producer are getting into a cab. She's not happy about it at all.

The next afternoon in the Plaza Santana, Harry is sitting at an outdoor cafe reading or at least looking at El Pais, a Spanish newspaper. On the table in front of him is a copy of a Spanish phrase book. Harry is smoking a cigar and sipping an espresso. Across the plaza, a distance of some thirty or forty yards away, a Spanish film crew is setting up for an interview: two chairs, a table and some flowers. A young female interviewer goes over her notes and talks to her director.

RJ approaches from a side street, spots Harry and joins him.

"Ah, there you are, old stain. Any luck?"

"Yeah, and it's all-bad. They have a list. It's not up to date and the guy we have to talk to about seeing it is out of town for the weekend. I did get the picture of Chase copied. Does this really look like him?"

"It's not a great picture, but yes."

"I doubt I'd recognize him. He looks like his mother though doesn't he?"

"In a way, I suppose. He also looks a bit like you.

Wakey, wakey! Anybody home?"

"What? Oh, sorry, I went somewhere else."

"I could see that. Do you do that often?"

"Do what?"

"Driftin' and dreamin'."

"Yeah, as a matter of fact I do. What's with the cigar?"

"Montecristo. Cuban. Can't get these in the states."

"I know. This going to be a new vice?"

"Not necessarily a new one. I have one of these occasionally on the island."

RJ waves the envelope he is carrying at the cigar smoke. RJ drops a paper envelope on the table and on top of that a picture of Chase.

"So, what do we do now?"

"I don't know. The traffic is unbelievable. Took me over an hour to get here. The peace conference parade is this evening. Maybe we rest up a little, try to see this golf federation guy tomorrow, and take it from there."

"Right. Sounds like a plan. Did you see this?"

He holds the paper for RJ to see the picture on page three. Another young man has been murdered.

"How many is that?"

"Well, my command of the language is practically non-existent, but I think that's number eleven."

"Something on your mind?"

"May I see that paper?"

RJ peruses the article about the serial killer. Across the plaza Jordan joins the interview crew. He is the subject of the piece.

Harry sees him and says, "Is that guy following us?"

"You're kidding."

"Who is he?"

"That's Jordan Christopher the TV news guy."

"Never heard of him. Been out of the country."

RJ returns to the newspaper.

"The police don't say what was used to strangle these guys. Don't they usually?"

"Like a nylon stocking or something?"

"Exactly. No mention in this article, as far as I can tell either."

"Maybe it's a...damn, I can't remember. You know when they hold back something from the public hoping to catch out the killer when they get him."

"Some piece of information only the killer would know about."

"Right. What's that called?"

"I don't know. Does it have a particular name?"

"Makes me crazy when I can't remember things."

"It's your age."

"Thank you."

"You're welcome."

"When did Chase disappear?"

"Shortly after the first of the year. Why?"

"Just curious. You said something about your being worried about his mental state. Was he suicidal?"

"Quite the opposite. Angry. At me. At himself. He seemed to suddenly have developed a very short fuse."

"Where are you going with this?"

"The first of these serial killings was on the nineteenth of February in Torremolinos…that's southern Spain. Golf country."

"Nonsense. Chase is not capable of such a thing."

After a while RJ says, "Tell me what happened to his mother."

"It's very complicated. And it's nothing like this other horrible thing with the young men. I'll tell you about it some other time."

"We've got nothing to do until Monday."

"Right. Well, up to a point, it was pretty much the way you thought it was. You blamed her for the death of your daughter."

"The pool didn't have an alarm system or a fence. Ginny was upstairs in bedroom with a boyfriend, according to the housekeeper, and no one was watching Callie. She fell into the pool and drowned. End of story. You know all of this."

"I do. And, as I remember your telling me, reason enough to kill her."

"A bad idea as it turned out and one I couldn't follow through with. So…?"

"So, Ginny had a drug problem. A big one. It was just a matter of time before she overdosed or managed to run through her considerable trust fund set up by her father with instructions that stated once that was gone she was on her own. She in turn had a will leaving her worldly goods to her children."

"Which, now that Callie is gone, would go to Chase."

"That's right. So, like you, we had a plan. After Ginny was out of the way, shall we say, we would use whatever was left to buy the hotel on the island."

"How nice. Even if it a tad cold-blooded."

"You want to hear this or not?"

"I used to think it was the only thing I wanted to hear. Now, I'm not so sure. But, go ahead."

"The night of the Halloween party … we were pretty certain, from what you had told me, that that was when you were going to, ah …"

"Shoot her."

"Right. Only you didn't. For whatever reason or reasons."

"Drank too much. Fell asleep. Wasn't capable of killing her in the first place … who knows?"

"Then later I telephoned you, after the party, and invited you to her house."

"For a glass of doped Champagne."

"The plan was … our plan … Chase and mine … was to wait until she passed out from too much cocaine and drop her into the swimming pool. Once we'd determined you weren't going ahead with your little shooting spree."

"That always seemed to me to be fraught with problems … a possible miss … hitting someone else … the noise…"

"So you dropped her into the pool and left me conked out in the living room for the cops to find. As they say; what are friends for?"

Jordan and Stacey seem very relaxed and comfortable with each other until Jordan sees an interviewer approaching from across the plaza. He whispers something to Stacey who leaves by a small side street in the other direction. Jordan, puts on his "charming hat" and stands to greet the interviewer a very attractive young woman who appears to be in her late twenties or early thirties. They shake hands and the interview begins.

"So, first off, has this rather special relationship, this friendship you have with the President afforded you any special privileges ... any access not available to the other members of the Washington press corps?"

"It's funny, but I think in an odd sort of way it's more of a hindrance than a benefit. The President is such an honorable man; such a believer in equality for everyone that I sometimes think our having been roommates in college has put me at a distinct disadvantage. I sometimes get the impression that if it wasn't for the way the First Lady and my wife get along I'd never see him at all."

In the background RJ and Harry are seen getting the check from a waiter and trying to figure it out.

"Besides I wasn't there."

"What?"

"When I left Ginny's house you were passed out in the living room and, as far as I knew, she in the same state, but still in her bed."

"Oh, come on."

"It's the truth. I had a change of heart. At the last minute I told Chase I couldn't go through with it and I left."

"You expect me to believe that?"

"That's entirely up to you, isn't it? I've done an awful lot of things in my life I'm not proud of, but I've never murdered anyone."

"So what you're telling me is that Chase murdered his mother all by himself?"

"No, I'm saying one can only surmise. Who knows maybe she woke up, came back thinking the party was still going on and fell into the pool."

"Oh, please, spare me."

"To get the full story you must find Chase."

RJ thinks about this for a moment and glances at the newspaper. A vendor walks by and places a flyer on their table.

"And this is the guy that you say is incapable of being a serial murderer. I wonder what a homicide detective would say about that."

"These two matters are entirely different. You forget what kind of a woman his mother was."

"Oh, no, I don't. I know exactly who and what she was. She'd bring out the killer instinct in a saint."

"Well, then you of all people should be able to see the difference between a young man who hates his mother and a crazed person who goes around strangling gay men."

"I'm working on it."

RJ looks at the flyer on the table. It is for a gay nightclub.

"Harry, did you and Chase ever hangout in these kinds of places?"

Harry looks at the flyer.

"Not as a matter of habit, but, yes, on occasion. Why do you ask?"

"Well, what are we looking for? A gay man, right?"

"Are you suggesting we start cruising gay bars?"

"Well, no, not we. You."

"Right. A man my age ... that doesn't speak more than a few words of Spanish ... is going to enter a gay bar and start asking questions. I don't think so. A waste of time and potentially dangerous. Now, if you care to come along and translate..."

"Oh, no, not me."

"And why not? Afraid you might feel threatened?"

The film crew is finishing pack up its gear. The interview is over. But, for Jordan, the intercourse is just beginning. As the crew moves off he moves his chair close to the interviewer turning on the charm full blast; his attentions are not rebuffed.

Much later that evening Jordan is standing in front of a backdrop of the city fully illuminated. We see various monitors showing each camera's picture along the parade route and the one on Jordan. A makeup person is doing last minute touch-ups. An assistant director says something to Jordan who nods his approval. Jordan turns and winks at Stacey.

On one of the monitors the cameraman is picking out various people from the crowd: babies being held by parents along the parade route, flags from around the world, etc. Music is blaring from loudspeakers. We see a glimpse of RJ and Harry working their way through the crowd.

"Here we go. In ten, nine, eight, seven, six, five, four, three. He indicates the last two seconds with his fingers and gives Jordan the "go" sign."

"Good evening from Madrid. We'll have the rest of today's headlines later in the program, but first we begin with the first day of what must surely be one of the more momentous days in modern history: the first world peace conference. A meeting of the world's leaders whose only agenda is peace and what they can do to help bring it about."

Various shots of the visiting dignitaries and heads of state including the President of the United States the only one in an open car.

"The first of the official ceremonies, the Parade of Peace began moments ago on the Paseo del Prado, one of Madrid's main arteries, which, as you may have guessed from the name, passes right in front of Madrid's most famous museum The Prado. Early this morning we were shocked to learn that, at the last moment, the President of the United States has opted to ride in an open car causing, needless to say, a security nightmare. But the President wants to send a very strong message: terrorists will not intimidate world leaders."

RJ and Harry are standing at the bar in a very crowded and very noisy disco. All men. RJ looks terribly uncomfortable. Harry, as one might suspect, seems to be enjoying himself: dancing in place, sipping a beer. RJ is constantly glancing around the room as if looking for someone. Which, of course, he is.

"I wish you wouldn't do that."

"What?"

"Looking around like that."

"What am I supposed to be doing? We're trying to find Chase, right?"

"Yes, but it looks like you're not satisfied being with me."

"Oh, for god's sake, Harry."

"Well, I'm sorry. I can't help it."

"Are you going to have a snit?"

"No, as a matter of fact, I'm not. I'm going to the loo."

"You wouldn't dare leave me here …Harry! Harry?"

Michael Bodkin reports from along the parade route.

"Even though they have not created an uproar, like they did two years ago when they shot and killed a young city councilman and his wife as they were walking home from the theatre, the possibility of an incident created by the extremist arm of the Basque separatist movement known as ETA is always a possibility. Jordan."

"Michael Bodkin along the parade route. We'll be back after this."

Back at the gay bar Harry is working his way through the crowd checking out a few buns in the process. RJ is not where he left him at the bar. Harry looks around the room and spots RJ talking to a young man at a table. RJ looks like he's enjoying himself. Harry joins them.

"Jason, this is my friend Harry. The guy I was telling you about. Harry … Jason."

"They shake hands."

"Jason speaks English. He works for IBM here in Madrid."

"Is that so? How nice."

"It's a living. Beats the hell out of New York, I'll tell you."

"I can imagine."

"Jason also spends a lot of time traveling … and he plays golf."

"Really? What's your handicap?"

"I'm about a six. I don't get to play that much. Got to make a living."

"You don't play that much and you're a six. God, I'd sell my own mother to be a six."

"I showed Jason Chase's picture. He's pretty sure he's seen him."

"We sponsored a little celebrity pro-am a couple of weeks ago in Sotogrande. I'm pretty sure I saw him there. Is he about a single digit handicap?"

"He could be if he's playing a lot."

"What do you think?"

171

"I think we ought to head south in the morning."

"Thanks, Jason, you've been a great help. May I buy you a drink?"

"Thanks, I've still got one working. I'm not much of a drinker. I wouldn't say no to a dance though."

RJ looks at Harry. This is exactly what he was afraid of. Harry just smiles.

Sometime later that evening RJ and Harry are hurrying along out of the parade crowd. Harry is slightly bemused. He is also lighting a cigar.

"Is it my imagination or are your cigars getting bigger?"

"Romeo y Julietta number five. Heaven."

"I'm thrilled for you."

"You were rather good back there in the club. I particularly liked that little thing you did with your hips."

"Harry…"

"Very sexy."

Harry…

"And I wasn't the only one."

"Harry…."

"Quite the little attention getter when you want to be, aren't you."

RJ stops suddenly and takes Harry's arm.

"Stop. Have you noticed anything peculiar?"

Harry's first response is to the previous conversation, but quickly realizes RJ has something else on his mind. As they both glance around they are immediately aware that the night is suddenly completely dark.

"No lights. Power failure?"

"Maybe. Not a single street light and no lights in any of the buildings. I wonder what's going on. Listen."

The fireworks are still going off but now there is the added sound of many, many police klaxons.

Mayhem. For some reason, even though there are no lights except the car headlights and flashlights belonging to the various security people, and the fireworks continue to light up the sky. Security agents have crammed themselves into the official cars, guns drawn, using their bodies to cover their charges. Sirens blare thru the darkness. A small group of young people has turned on a boom box and are dancing on the sidewalk oblivious to what is going on around them.

Inside the temporary Broadcast News set almost total darkness. Although someone has found a flashlight. Jordan is still sitting at his news desk. Stacey brings him a small bottle of water.

"What the hell is going on?"

The stage manager says, "I don't know. It looks like the whole city's dark. Maybe a blackout. Phones for some reason are still working. We're trying to find out what happened."

"Thank god I wasn't in an elevator."

"That happen to you before?"

"The big one in Acapulco. Me, six other guys, and a large dog for five hours."

A darkened street outside another gay disco. Men can be heard laughing on the street and somewhere in the background one young man runs laughing into the alley and unzips his fly. He is still laughing as he pees. Suddenly, from behind him, a multi-colored cord slips around his neck and he is strangled. Gloved hands drop the ends of the cord. The assailant fumbles around in the dark, but can't find the murder weapon. Hearing voices approach he hurries off into the darkness.

On the news set it is till dark. The fireworks have finally stopped. Just the one flashlight in the studio.

Jordan calls out, "Can we get some air in here? Open a window or something. The air conditioning must be off."

Someone opens the main door leading to the makeshift studio and smoke comes billowing in. Someone else yells, "Fire! Close that door!" Jordan is talking to a producer and looks up just as a group of bomberos, members of the Madrid fire department, come bolting through the door with fire extinguishers and axes in hand.

"That was quick."

"Yeah, how'd they do that?"

"I don't know and frankly I don't care. Let's get the hell out of here."

Jordan grabs Stacey by the elbow and begins ushering her towards the door.

"Ladies and gentleman, please. There is a fire in the building and we cannot use the elevators because of the fire and the blackout. We want each of you to hold onto this rope and follow the bomberos down the stairs. It is very dark and smoky, but the fire itself is in another part of the building. Please move quickly and cover your mouths and noses with whatever you have."

Everyone does as instructed. Someone tries to get Jordan to go first, but he insists on waiting until the very last. They head down the dark, smoke filled stairway.

On the parade route someone has thrown smoke grenades at the car containing one of the Spanish politicians. Armed men in masks try to pull him from the car. A guard is shot at but missed. Eventually the terrorists retreat empty handed.

One by one the news crew comes staggering, red-eyed and coughing on to the street and begin collecting themselves.

"Boy, I never want to go through that again."

"You and me both."

The producer looks around the assembled crowd of onlookers and news personnel.

"I wonder where all the firemen went."

"Back into the building maybe."

"How do you suppose they got here so fast?"

"I don't know. Somebody called them."

"No, I mean … how. Did they walk? Do you see a fire truck anywhere? Fire hoses?"

They both look around their immediate area. Stacey seems terribly confused and seems to be looking for something.

"That's not all that's missing. Where's Jordan?"

Four men are in a car working its way through the streets of Madrid. Five men actually. Jordan is lying face down, hands and feet tied, a black hood over his head, on the floor in the back seat of the car. The two men in the rear have their feet on his back. They are all dressed very conservatively in dark suits and ties and they all are smoking and looking very tense. The driver of the car is a very large man with a huge mustache.

The next day in New York a meeting is taking place in the office of Managing Editor Don Forrester of the news department. A dozen or more producers and department heads are listening and talking to a producer on the speakerphone from Madrid. A woman in her late fifties storms into the room. It is Jordan's wife Dixie. She starts to say something and is stopped by the upraised hand of the Editor. "I just don't have the answer to that, Don. All I can tell you is what the local police are telling me. There were no firemen sent to our building and there was no fire. Just a couple of smoke bombs under the stairwell."

"What about any calls or letters to the newspapers or television stations claiming responsibility?"

"One to El Pais, one of the national papers. Some guy called and said he was a member of ETA and they had nothing to do with it. He said, however, that they were the ones that tried to kidnap the local guy. The cops don't know whether to believe him or not."

"All right, Jerry. Call me again in two hours or sooner if anything develops."

"One other thing, for what it's worth. Let's hope this caller was on the level and ETA doesn't have Jordan. They're notorious for keeping their victims for forty-eight hours and them killing them and leaving the bodies in a park somewhere."

Dixie is trying hard not react to this piece of news. Forrester hangs up the phone and moves to her and motions her to the couch.

"I'm sorry you had to hear that, Dix. How are you doing?"

"I've never been so frightened in my life. I've worried for years that something awful like this would happen to Jordan, but when he moved into the anchor spot I thought I could finally relax. No more nasty little wars. No more…"

She loses it. Forrester signals the rest of the people out of the room and sits next to her on the couch.

"I'm going to move into a hotel until we find him. I saw more familiar faces camped outside the house this morning. It looked like a reunion of a lot of Bob's old friends. I just don't want to get caught up in a media circus."

"I wonder if a hotel is such a good idea. They're bound to find you sooner or later. Why don't you move in with us until this is over? We've got plenty of room and Penny always says we never see you anymore."

The door to Forrester's office opens and a woman sticks her head in.

"The President is on line one."

Forrester moves back to his desk and picks up the phone.

"Good morning, Mr. President."

He listens for a moment.

"I understand, Mr. President. She's sitting right here. (Listens) Of course."

He turns on the speakerphone.

"Dixie?"

She has moved to a chair closer to the phone.

"Good morning, Mr. President. How are you, John?"

"I'm very upset and angry. I'm also feeling exceedingly helpless. It doesn't appear we're any closer to finding Jordan then when we were when I left Madrid."

"Do you have any news for us?"

"Dixie, honey, I'm sorry. I wish I did. I wish I did."

"Don, you heard about the ETA phone call to El Pais?"

"Just a few moments ago."

"What do you make of it?"

"I don't know. If ETA doesn't have him, who does? And why?"

"Pretty much our thinking here as well. I've got to get back to a meeting. Let's stay in close contact, Don. And Dixie I want you to know we're doing everything we possibly can. We'll get him back. I promise you. He's still the best roommate I ever had."

He hangs up. Dixie and Forrester are both drained. They just stare at each other. "What's to be done?"

Jordan, whose head is still covered and whose hands are still tied behind him, is being led by two masked men along a darkened hallway. They enter a room that has a mattress on the floor, a straight-backed chair, and a bare light bulb overhead. The one window is sealed with a plastic tarp and the drapes are drawn. They push Jordan into the chair and strap him to it.

When they are finished and have double-checked his bounds and the window they leave. Even though he senses it is futile Jordan strains at his bindings to no avail.

Inside a fashionable New York restaurant Forrester and another man are seated at a table set for three people. Forrester looks tense, uneasy. He keeps looking around the restaurant hoping not to see anyone he recognizes. He sips a Martini straight up. The man, who could be a banker by the looks of his wardrobe, is relaxed, at ease, and sips coffee. There is a below the surface toughness about him that is not readily apparent. One suspects he has a "story."

Forrester says, "This business with Jordan has been the hardest thing I've ever been involved in. I guess it's because he's a friend and he's really the voice of the industry in a way."

Both men notice Dixie approaching with the maître d'. They rise to greet her. Forrester puts on his "game" face.

Forrester, kissing Dixie on the cheek says, "Lovely as ever. How are you, Dixie?"

"Thirsty." And then before Forrester can introduce them says, "Hi, I'm Dixie Jordan. Who are you?"

"Cal Mifflin, Mrs. Jordan, it's a pleasure meeting you ... even considering the circumstances."

"And what do you do Mr. Mifflin. May I call you Cal?"

"Of course you may."

Dixie fumbles in her purse for her cigarettes and motions for a waiter who scurries over and lights her cigarette.

"Thank you." Indicating Forrester, "I'll have whatever he's having. Make it a double and hurry."

Then back to the men at the table.

"Every tabloid rag and nut case in the entire country is after me. My husband has seemingly disappeared off the face of the planet. My son is acting very peculiarly. Phone calls in the middle of the night. Mysterious packages from companies I've never heard of. God knows what he's up to. He says it's all for a school project. Fat chance. So to answer your question; I'm fine. Just peachy. Having a wonderful time. So, Cal, you haven't told me, to what do I owe this … whatever it is?"

"Dixie, Cal's with a private counterinsurgency company headquartered in London. They're in the so-called K and R business. Kidnap and ransom."

"There's a kidnap and ransom business? Is that how you're listed in the yellow pages?"

"They help families and corporations negotiate the release of kidnap victims."

"I'm a little perplexed. Did you or did you not tell me the network was unwilling to negotiate with terrorists?"

"That's true I did. This is my own idea. The board of directors at the network doesn't know anything about it. I met Cal some time ago on another matter and I thought he might be able to be of some assistance regarding Jordan. His company has been at this in hundreds of cases around the world."

The waiter arrives with Dixie's drink from which she takes a healthy slug.

"Oh, that's good. Think I might just survive. Might not be the best choice of words under the circumstances."

"I'm concerned about what you said about your son. Headstrong teenaged boys can be a problem. Save his father. Be a hero to the family. That sort of thing. If you should decide to utilize my company's services we'd want to keep a close eye on his activities. Amateurs can be very dangerous."

"I'm sure."

"I don't want to bore you, but I think it might be helpful to you to hear some fast statistics. After some sort of negotiations roughly sixty-six percent of all victims are released. Only twenty-five percent were rescued or escaped."

"If my math is correct that leaves another ten percent. What happened to them? Maybe I don't want to know."

"They were either killed or died in captivity. My point is the chances of getting your husband back through the work of professional negotiators is better than two to one."

"I got it."

"Look, I think I'd better go. The less I know about all this the better. Dixie, why don't you call me later or, better yet, let's get together in a day or two and see where we are. I'm meeting with the board again on Wednesday. Maybe I'll have some news. I'll call you at your hotel."

Forrester sips the dregs of his drink, kisses Dixie, and shakes Mifflin's hand as he hurriedly exits the restaurant.

"He can wiggle out of a tight spot better than any man alive."

"He's in a very difficult position."

"I'm sorry, for that. You're right, of course. It's just so… I don't know."

"A man by the name of Thomas Hargrove, a Texan who was abducted in Columbia in 1994, I believe it was, said that kidnapping was the deliberate creation and marketing of human grief, anguish, and despair."

"Well, that certainly makes me feel a lot better. Waiter!"

LA CALA is an upscale golf resort on La Costa del Sol not far from Fuengirola. RJ and Harry are at the driving range hitting balls. Harry does very well. He has a nice slow swing. RJ, on the other hand, is fighting it all the way.

"Swing easy. Hit hard. Good advice from Julius Boros."

"Yeah, yeah."

"They say golf is a metaphor for life."

"Crap."

RJ tries another ball hitting it even harder. He tops it and it goes twenty yards.

"Maybe we should try the putting green."

They pick up their bags and move off.

"Harry, has it occurred to you that we just might be on a wild goose chase?"

"Is that a pun?"

"What?"

"Chasing Chase."

"Oh. It didn't start out that way. Look, we can go on like this forever. How many golf courses do you think there are in Spain and we're not even sure he's in this country. He also speaks English. He could be in Scotland or Ireland, for god's sake."

"It's different there. More of a traditional thing. Older pros. Cold weather. Not the kind of place he would like."

"You're probably right."

They move on to the putting green. From the area of the club house a young man in a hotel uniform approaches them.

"Mr. McCaw?"

"Yes?"

"I'm glad I found you. You have a phone call. He's says it's important."

RJ and Harry hurry to the clubhouse. They leave their bags in the rack and another man hands RJ the phone and punches up a line.

"Hello. This is RJ McCaw."

"RJ, it's Jason McGinley. We met in Madrid at the club."

"Jason. Right. I remember. How are you?"

"I'm fine, thank you. Listen, RJ, regarding that golf pro you're looking for … have you found him?"

"No not yet. We're still looking."

"Well, I don't know if this any help or not, but I went back through the list of players in that tournament I told you about that we sponsored."

"Yes …"

"And I found an address for a pro by the name of Chasin Sanborn. Could this be the guy you're looking for?"

RJ gives Harry a thumbs up and pantomimes needing a pencil and paper.

"That's him. Let me get something to write with."

Harry hands RJ a scorecard and a pencil.

"Okay, go ahead."

"It's Calle Serrano number twenty-one in Marbella. That's all I have. Evidently he wasn't affiliated with a club at that time. He may have had some kind of sponsor exemption."

"Jason, I can't thank you enough. Say, how'd you find me?"

"When we were in the bar the other night you mentioned you were heading south. La Cala was the logical place. Best course on the Med for my money. Also, you might be interested in knowing there was a policeman here in the office yesterday asking me about you and Harry. I told him about our conversation. I hope I haven't caused you any grief."

"Not at all. We're not doing anything illegal. Just looking for a friend."

"Well, I gotta' run. Good luck."

"Thanks, Jason. I really appreciate this."

RJ hangs up and looks to Harry.

"Marbella."

The next morning Harry and RJ are in the car looking for and an address and a place to park.

Axiom: wherever you go in Spain there never is a place to park. So, when in Rome do as the romans do. RJ pulls the car up onto the sidewalk, turns off the engine and the two of them get out. They walk a ways until they come to Number 21; a small, whitewashed apartment building with a courtyard. They enter and encounter a sixtyish woman coming towards them with a small, very old dog.

"Perdona me, señora, yo mirado por un hombre …"

Then too RJ: "How do you say …"

The woman who speaks with a British accent says, "Would it help you to speak English?"

"Ah, yes, a great deal, thank you, dear lady. My name is Neville Churchill and this is my friend RJ McCaw. We're looking for RJ's son and we're told he may be living here."

RJ gives him a look at the mention of Churchill.

"No, no one by the name of McCaw. Sorry."

"Well, thank you anyway."

They turn to leave.

"That wouldn't be Mr. Sanborn you're looking for?"

"Yes, yes it is. It's, ah, long story about the different last names."

"I understand. Well, unfortunately, he's not here."

"Do you have any idea when he might be returning?"

"I should think never. He left two, or was it three, weeks ago. His rent is paid until the first of next month, but from the looks of his apartment I don't think he'll be coming back."

"I see. Did he leave a forwarding address of any kind?"

"No. Nothing at all. Just some books and papers. Nothing of any real value. Since you're his father you're welcome to look around, if you like. We're just on the way to the market. The doors unlocked. Just close it when you leave. Top of the stairs. First door on your right."

She and the dog head for the street.

"Thank you so much."

They climb the stairs.

"Neville Churchill? You can't be serious."

"You'd be surprised how many doors it opens. Case in point."

They enter the apartment. A simply decorated place. Light and airy. Sparse. Harry starts looking through some correspondence. RJ concentrates on a few old, dog-eared books.

"Anything there?"

"Doesn't look like it. Receipts mostly."

RJ is looking over the books. The titles include: SECRETS OF METHAMPHETAMINE ... Recipes for MDA, ECSTASY and other PSYCHEDELIC AMPHETAMINES. HUXLEY AND GOD by Aldus Huxley and LAS PLANTAS FUMABLES.

"What do you make of these?"

Harry pockets what he is looking at and examines the books.

"Think he's still into drugs?"

"Then why would he leave these?"

"I don't know. They look pretty dog-eared. Maybe he got some new ones."

RJ and Harry get back into the car. From a doorway a man in a suit, tie and sunglasses is smoking a cigarette and watching them.

Sitting in the rental car RJ and Harry are both locked into their own thoughts for a few moments.

"You know, it occurs to me that if this woman knows something about Chase perhaps others do to."

"For instance?"

"Well, he had to eat. Do laundry. Have fun."

"I'm not cruising in any more gay bars."

"Too bad. You're so good at it."

RJ and Harry spend the day showing Chase's picture around Marbella: restaurants, cleaners, grocery stores, golf shops, etc. Harry periodically consults his Spanish language phrase book.

RJ and Harry enter a restaurant in Fuengirola a beach area not far from Marbella. Harry suddenly seems very ill at ease. As they follow a waiter to a table they overhear a conversation between two elderly British men.

"My wife died very young"

"I wasn't that fortunate."

The man who we saw outside Chase's old apartment also enters the restaurant and takes a seat at the end of the bar.

"God, I need a drink."

Harry signals to a waiter who immediately comes to their table.

"Un agua sin gas y una gin tonic para me. RJ?"

"The same, por favor."

The waiter leaves. The boys look at each other.

"Now what?"

"I wish I knew. It appears we're back to square one. It doesn't look like he's here. No one recognizes his picture. Odd, to say the least. Let's go."

"Hang on. We just ordered a drink."

Reluctantly Harry settles into his chair. He is suddenly very edgy. He keeps twitching and looking around the room.

"What's the matter with you? You look like a six year old who has to go to the bathroom."

"Nothing. I'm fine. I just remembered I've been in this place before … a long time ago … that's all."

The waiter comes with the drinks. As he is placing them on the table an old man comes shuffling into the bar. He is walking with a cane and has a newspaper and a stack of letters and writing materials in his hands. One of the bartenders says 'hola' to him and the old man sits at 'his table' in a corner of the bar. Harry sees him.

"Oh, god, I was afraid of this."

He slugs his drink and reaches into his pocket for some money.

"Let's get out of here."

RJ has figured out that the old man has something to do with Harry's agitation.

"Harry, what's going on?"

They haven't noticed that the man who has been following them has approached their table. The man sits down without waiting to be asked.

"May I join you?"

Harry is now doubly irritated.

"It looks like you already have."

"You will, please, excuse my impertinence; I am trying to be as unobtrusive as possible."

"A cop, I'd wager."

"How did you know that?"

"A lucky guess. What can we do for you?"

The Man shows them some identification.

"My name is Camarena. I'm with the National Police. I believe we are all looking for the same man. A Mister Sanborn."

"Perhaps…"

"Let's not be coy with each other. We know who you are Mr. RJ McCaw and Mr. Neville Churchill … perhaps, is it Señor MacDivitt … or is it Mr. Hyde these days?"

"I see."

"I sincerely hope so."

"Look, let's cut to the chase…"

"A joke?"

"Wasn't meant to be. We're merely trying to find … my son. That's all there is to it. I assume you're trying to find him also or why would you interested in us."

"There have been a number of seemingly related murders."

"Yes, we know. We read the newspapers."

"And we are looking into a number of possibilities as to the identification of the killer or killers. One of which is the idea that perhaps this person is a homosexual himself."

"And so you're checking up on all the male homosexuals in the country? Seems like an impossible task."

"The Spanish have a lot of experience in this area."

"Careful."

"Good advice. Well, I must be going now."

"Wait just a minute. What was the purpose of this? Are you trying to intimidate us?"

"Not at all. I'm just letting you know we are aware of your presence and, perhaps, to warn you to be very careful. What happens if you find this man before we do and he turns out to be the killer? What then?"

"He's not a murderer. I … we know him and…."

"How well do we ever know someone? The happily married man who collects dirty pictures. The wealthy woman who shop lifts. Who would have guessed?"

He gets up to leave and takes a calling card out of his pocket.

"You never know. Take my card. It might come in … what's the word?"

"Handy."

"Yes. Handy. Good-bye."

Camarena leaves. RJ and Harry stare at each other.

"Hyde?"

"My real name. Now you see why I changed it."

"Does this make me Doctor Jekyll? Doctor Jekyll and Harry Hyde?"

"I don't think so."

RJ thinks this is pretty funny.

"'Ello, 'ello. 'Oim 'Arry 'Yde from 'Ampstead 'Eep."

"All right, that's enough."

"Whatever you say, 'Arry …"

"RJ!"

"Okay, okay. So, now what?"

"I think it's time we got the hell out of Marbella."

"I agree, but where to?"

Harry takes a matchbook out of his pocket and hands it to RJ.

"I found this in Chase's old room."

"Hotel El Puerto Mundaka? Where's Mundaka?"

"Northwestern Spain. Not far from San Sebastain as I remember."

"Okay, let's head out first thing in the morning. I'm beat. I'm turning in early."

"Let's get something to eat and then head back to La Cala."

Later that same evening Harry has returned to the bar where he and RJ talked to the cop. The old man was still there although he had moved from the table where he was and seemed to be writing letters to the bar. Still with a beer and no signs of having eaten. Harry watches him for a while, starts to approach him, changes his mind and flees.

An apartment complex somewhere in Spain. Police cars arrive outside the building and masked officers dressed in black outfits and carrying automatic weapons ascend the stairs. They break into an apartment and toss a smoke grenade. Gunfire immediately erupts. It appears that at least two of the inhabitants are killed.

The exterior of the Spanish apartment building right after the raid. Prisoners are being escorted into a police van their arms handcuffed behind them and their heads covered with white hoods.

Tom Kelley is the new anchor temporarily replacing Jordan. He is a very interesting looking man in his mid-forties. He has many of the same qualities we associated with all network anchors and he is a good deal younger than most.

On the news that evening Kelley says, "A source inside the special Spanish task force created to try and find I.B.C.'s Jordan Christopher says no trace of the missing anchor has been uncovered. However, the police spokesman said three suspected ETA terrorists were killed, fifteen more were arrested, and an entire wing of the separatist group was broken up."

On the autopista heading north RJ is driving and Harry has a map on his lap and he is reading a Spanish newspaper.

"There's a story in today's paper about some British guy in Seville who had three triple Scotches before dinner, two bottles of red wine with dinner and several brandies afterward. Then he went back to his hotel room and drank the entire contents of his mini-bar."

"Jesus. How did he survive all that booze?"

"He didn't. Dead. A maid found him the next afternoon."

Harry continues scanning the paper … then puts it down and stares out the window.

"You want to tell me about him?"

"No."

"You don't even know…"

"The old guy back in the bar in Fuengirola was my father."

"I see."

"I doubt it. He's a drunk. Should have been dead years ago. All he does is drink Guinness and write letters to the few remaining members of his family or god knows who. Pathetic. Never eats. Used to drink regular Spanish draft beer. Any kind. Then he switched to

Guinness because he thinks because it's thicker it has more food value. Crazy. Being Irish helps."

"How come you got so agitated when you saw him?"

"We don't get along. It's just that simple. He doesn't like me and frankly I'm scared to death of him. Always have been and I guess I always will be. I went back to the bar last night. Thought we could have a chat. You know, catch up. Couldn't do it. Just stood there and stared at him. Felt like my feet were encased in cement and I was just waiting to be thrown overboard. Eventually he finished whatever he was doing, packed up and left the bar. Didn't see him pay. Maybe he runs a tab. Anyway, he left the bar and after a few minutes…giving him a head start, I followed him out, but he was nowhere to be seen. Disappeared. Nowhere in sight. Just like he always did when I was a kid. Here today. Gone today. A missed opportunity and I was so relieved."

"What did he do to you?"

"It's not so much what he's done as who he is. He's a bastard. He's sarcastic, competitive… but only with men he views as a threat…like me. He's relentlessly contemptuous of just about everything. Extraordinarily confrontational. He'll take the opposite side of an argument even though he believes in the other side, just to be a prick. He once said to my mother that he felt he had to be a son of a bitch at least three times a day or he wasn't happy. As a kid I'd get so angry with him I'd run out of a room in tears. Once he's on your back he stays there forever or until you manage to get away from him as I did. Oh, well…"

"Whew! That's a mouthful. What about your mother? Where is she?"

"Dead. Died of an overdose years ago. I think she did it just to get away from him. I saw him, oh, maybe fifteen years ago. Looked him up. He seemed different, somehow. He said, 'I love you, son.' First time he'd ever told me that. I asked him why he thought he loved me and he had no answer."

They ride on for a while in silence. Harry returns to his newspaper.

"I saw him again some time later in Paris. I almost didn't recognize him. A beard. Long hair. An old fedora. A dark sweater that had seen better days. And an easel, a paint box, brushes, the whole deal. The strange thing was he was standing half on the sidewalk and half in the street and get this: he was painting a nude statue, you know, like those things, whatever they're called, you see of a little boy pissing in a swimming pool. Around the base of the statue were absolutely gorgeous roses. Get this: every once in a while he would look up from the canvas as if he was taking a look at the scene he was painting only he was on a street with no little boys, no statue, and no flowers. Weird."

They ride on in silence for a while before Harry says, "Listen to this. There is a thing called a brain hook. It was used for removing the brain, in hunks, through the back of the nose. The Egyptians invented it to preserve the pharaoh's."

"Gruesome."

Harry continues leafing through the paper. "I find that sometimes your insecurity can be overwhelming."

"What's that supposed to mean?"

"It's a quote from a book review. It's the kind of thing my father would say to me."

Later Harry is driving and smoking an even bigger cigar. RJ is in the back seat gazing out the window. Harry continues rattling on.

"Essentially we, that is, science, went in the wrong direction. We became so enamored with Einstein and his relativity theory that we became transfixed with getting there physically. Wherever 'there' might be. We should have been trying to travel mentally. Teleportation and telecommunication make much more sense. That's what flying saucers do. They don't travel they just appear."

RJ continues looking out the window.

Still later RJ is back to driving and Harry is stretched out on the back seat and still talking.

"So, if a man's life is like the face of a clock how much time does he have left when the hands are at seven-thirty?"

Harry in now driving and RJ is in the back.

"Not that either. No thanks."

"I wasn't making an offer."

"What about with the other thing?"

RJ contemplates: what's he referring to. "Oh, yeah. That."

"Ever try it with a girlfriend?"

Harry seems to like getting to RJ and making him uncomfortable.

"No, not really."

"'No not really?' There's a qualified answer if I ever heard one. Anal, oral; a man and a woman. Anal, oral; a man and a man. Anal oral, a woman and a woman. We're all doing the same things, right? So, what's the big deal anyway?"

Still much later both men are in the front of the car. RJ is driving. A sign reads Mundaka. 25 kilometers. There are traveling along a road that parallels a river. The scene is so pretty that even Harry is finally quiet.

In her hotel room in New York Dixie is putting some fresh dry cleaning away and talking on the phone. There is a knock at the door.

"Bobby, there isn't anything you can do. Just try to be patient and don't talk to the press. Hold on a second there's someone at the door."

She lets a room service waiter in. He is carrying a drink tray, which he puts down on the cocktail table. He hands her a slip of paper, which she assumes is the bill for her to sign. She looks at it and doesn't immediately understand.

"Two million dollars? What's this?

Bobby, honey, I'll call you back. I have to go. Bye, sweetie."

"Who are you?"

"It doesn't matter who I am."

He heads for the door.

"You have three days. Two million dollars. Cash. No markings. No police or your husband is dead."

"Wait, please. My husband. How is he?"

"He is fine. He's even put on a little weight. We'll be in touch."

He leaves. Dixie stands looking at the note. There is another knock at the door. It is Dixie and Jordan's son Bobby; a handsome seventeen years old.

"Hi, Mom, what's happening?"

"Dixie glances at the phone. How did you get here so fast?"

"I called from the lobby Are you all right? What's that?"

Before she can reply Bobby snatches the note out of her hand and reads it.

"Two million dollars? Where are we going to get two million dollars?"

"It shouldn't be all that difficult. It's not like we're paupers. Your father is one of the highest paid men in the business."

"I know, but three days?"

Forrester and Dixie are walking through Central Park. It is a gray, dreary day.

"Not a clue. I talked with the President a few hours ago. No news. He said we have some undercover people throughout Spain doing the best they can. No one, even some contacts inside ETA, have any idea where he might be. There is even some speculation he's...."

"Don't say it. He's not dead."

"That's not what I was going to say. There's been some conjecture in Madrid that he was abducted by some group not associated with ETA at all. ETA almost always makes a phone call confirming responsibility for the act. Not this time. Not a word."

"So what's that all mean?"

"As far as we're concerned absolutely nothing. I'm sorry to say we're no closer to finding him than we were three weeks ago."

"What about the board meeting?"

"They are still adamant: no negotiations with or money for terrorists. Have you heard anything from Cal Mifflin's people?"

"They've given me a lot of very useful information. They talked to Bobby and I think they've convinced him to stay out of it. At least I hope so. Other than that... nothing. Did you see The Star?"

"With that grisly picture of the mutilated body on the cover? We had a photo analysis done. It's not Jordan. It might not even be a man."

"That's what I thought, but it wasn't the picture I was referring to. You don't have to say anything. This isn't the first of Jordan's little indiscretions. She's very attractive, isn't she?"

"I..."

"You men ... you're all such bad boys. You should all be spanked."

Dixie walks on. Forrester eventually catches up with her.

"He'll turn up. I know he will. We've been through a lot of tough stuff together. I won't let this happen."

She walks on. It appears she is wrestling with a problem.

"I got a note last night at the hotel. God knows how they found out I was staying there. They want two million dollars."

Forrester stops walking and watches Dixie as she starts to continue on. He has a puzzled look on his face.

"Dixie you not seriously considering…"

She stops and turns to him.

"What do you think? Of course I am. Your board and our government might not negotiate with terrorists, but I sure the hell will. Anything… anything to get him back."

"Dixie…"

She doesn't appear to hear him and resumes walking, faster this time.

"Dixie, please!"

In his cell, a dark room with only a cot and a thunder mug, Jordan is managing to untie himself. First the hands, then the ankles. He stands up and walks stiffly to the window, which is still covered with a black curtain. He pulls back the curtain to find the opening has been boarded up. There is, however, a small space between two of the planks. On the other side in the distance quite a ways away he can see: a grassy slope covered with trees. Trees. Trees. And more trees.

Suddenly on the other side of the opening the partial face of the large mustachioed lead kidnapper appears.

"Chico!"

Seconds later the huge guard named Chico bursts into the room. He is wearing a black hood as a precaution. He knocks Jordan down with a single punch to the body and stands over him waiting for orders as the mustachioed man enters the room. Jordan fights to get his breath.

"Tie him. Tight this time and watch him like you would the money in your pocket. If he tries anything hit him with the pipe."

The I.B.C. NEWS set. Tom Kelley with the news. "The President also said in his press conference...the first since his return from Madrid ...that there is still no word on the whereabouts of I.B.C. anchor Jordan Christopher.

In an unrelated story out of Bogotá, Columbia, the corpse of another missing journalist, Jaime Alejandro of El Tiempo, the country's leading daily, was found last night in the southwest of the country. Sources at El Tiempo confirmed that pieces of his body had been turning up in and around Bogotá for the last week or so."

In a very large and well equipped kitchen Jordan is sitting on a straight-backed wooden chair. His hands and feet are bound and he has a black blindfold around his head covering his eyes. A television set is on and Tom Kelley is finishing the story about the South American newsman.

Behind Jordan a man says, "In some parts of the world journalists are an endangered species."

Jordan's body reacts to this as if he had been shot. The man behind Jordan is perhaps named Hillario. He is very tall and has an enormous handlebar mustache and holds a large knife and is chopping peppers and onions. He is making a salad which includes anchovies, tuna, and hard-boiled eggs. A fish is on a grill behind him and the fire is creating a lot of smoke.

"I saw a piece on the B.B.C. news last night on you. Everyone seems to think this guy Kelly who is taking your place is very good. Very good looking also."

Jordan squirms a little.

"He looks a little like you did a long time ago."

Jordan squirms even more. Hillario continues preparing the food. Another man, even bigger than Hillario, stands behind Jordan guarding.

"I understand the network's ratings are way up since you've been enjoying your stay with us. Maybe they won't want you back. Bad news for you. Bad news for us. We're counting on a lot of big bucks to turn you over. If we don't get it this guy Kelly is going to have a permanent position."

"My people won't submit to any demands from some half-assed terrorists. You and the rest of your ETA buddies will rot in hell before you get a dime."

"Hey, we're not terrorists. I hate those ETA bastards. We got nothing to do with them."

"Right. How silly of me. You're just doing this to create a little good will between our two countries."

"Not quite. We need some money to start a restaurant."

Hillario tends to the fish.

"You can't be serious."

"That's the truth. We got a friend inside ETA who told us they were going to create some disruptions during the peace parade in Madrid. So we borrowed some bombero's stuff … you know what is bombero's? … firemen … and took you for a little vacation."

"I don't believe you."

"That's okay, you don't have to, but that's it. ETA's getting pretty pissed off. All these cops and army guys breaking into their houses looking for you. ETA don't know where you are any more than they do. Pretty funny, no?"

"Hilarious."

"Hey, that's my name … Hillario. And I'm from a small village called Hillaria."

"I don't think you'd be telling me all this if that was you're real name."

Hillario is transferring the cooked fish to a wooden serving plank.

"Maybe not. Are you hungry? I got a nice piece of merluza here. Grilled over a wood fire with garlic and salt. Fantastic. Going to serve it just like this, a la plancha, in my new restaurant."

Jordan's body language indicates that he is suddenly very hungry.

RJ and Harry arrive in Mundaka, a very small and very pretty pueblo where the Atlantic Ocean meets the river that flows north from Guernica. On the palisade there is a lovely church that overlooks a long stretch of beach; a surfer paradise. Nearby is a small port with twenty or so old fashioned, two man-fishing boats. The Hotel El Puerto is the only lodging in the immediate area. Next to the hotel is graffiti painted on a white wall which reads: 'without the truth you are the loser.'

RJ and Harry leave their baggage in the car and walk through the little park to the edge of the cliff. The sun is setting. The locals are walking their dogs. It is the evening paseo. Harry and RJ are weary from a long day of driving. They stop and gaze out over the water.

"Pretty place."

"Gorgeous."

They continue walking.

"After a certain age it becomes readily apparent you'll probably never visit certain places ever again.

And you won't play quarterback for the Packers either."

"You know, I truly believe I've mellowed on this trip."

"Mellowed, Harry? In your case it's probably just a phase."

RJ finds himself momentarily trapped in Harry's melancholy.

"We've missed a lot, you know. No kids in our lives. Not even a pet cat."

"You had a child."

"Yes, but for such a short time."

They walk along a bit further, each engrossed in their own thoughts. Twenty or thirty yards in front of them a little girl strolling with her mother sees her father, a fisherman, walking up the stairs from the harbor. She starts running toward him a big smile on her face.

RJ's mind reverts to the past in Florida. RJ'S daughter Callie is struggling having fallen into a swimming pool and, being unable to swim, drowns. Raggedy Ann floats nearby. RJ is used to these memory flashes having experienced them many times in one form or another over the years. He is abruptly pulled back to reality by Harry's voice.

"I had a dog once. When I was a very little boy. A Pekinese."

"I hate those things. Peeks and Chihuahua's."

Harry, undeterred says, "This dog was very special. Terribly, terribly, sensitive. We called her Sylvia. My mother thought she looked like Sylvia Sydney."

"Who?"

"Oh, come now, surely you can't be too young to remember…"

Harry realizes, from the smile on RJ's face that he's been had and doesn't like it one bit.

"Very funny. I'm not that much older than you. Oh well, you know no matter how hard I try, I just can't stay mad at you, RJ, my boy."

"Don't be too concerned, Harry. The important thing is you tried."

They return to watching the sun set.

"A good place to stand and look at God."

"You never fail to surprise me, Harry."

"Me, too."

"Do you have a philosophy about yourself, Harry?"

"I do indeed. To quote Popeye…"

"Popeye? The sailor man?"

"Indeed, the very same. He always said, "I yam what I yam.""

Spanish police dressed in military style clothing and wearing masks are surrounding a house somewhere in Spain that has a light burning in only one room in the back. One of the policemen tries to see though the window, but it is covered with a drape. He signals this to the others. Another cop takes out a tool and very quietly prises open the exterior door.

Once inside the policemen make their way noiselessly to a door with light showing under it.

The leader makes a show of three fingers. Two of the cops line up to break down the door. On the count of three one of them hits the old door with his boot sending it right off its rusted hinges clattering to the floor.

Inside a small, thin, elderly man stands in front of a full-length mirror. He is wearing a bullfighter's traje de luces … suit of lights … including the small black hat. Over the costume he wears a bra, panties, a garter belt and long black stockings. Not exactly what the cops expected to find.

A telephone is ringing in RJ's room in the Mundaka hotel. Slow to wake and realize where he is RJ reaches for the phone which has finally stopped ringing.

"Hello? Hello?"

Too late. Whoever it was has hung up. RJ makes his way to the bathroom, takes a pee, washes his face and heads back to the bedroom where he notices a slip of paper stuck under the door.

"Tried calling, but guess you were out or sleeping late. Didn't want to disturb you. Gone to find the golf course and check it out. Maybe hit some balls. Back for lunch. H."

RJ drops the note on a table and staggers back to bed. But, something is jarring his memory. He goes back to the bathroom, throws some water on his face, brushes his teeth, and dries his face all the while trying to remember… something. He opens his briefcase and extracts the note Harry had given him back in the States that was from Chase. RJ examines the two pieces of paper. They are obviously written by the same hand.

Much later that morning RJ is having a coffee on the veranda outside the hotel. He has the notes in front of him.

Harry comes walking up carrying his golf clubs and a shoe bag.

"Morning, old stain. Sleep well?"

RJ flips him the notes.

"What's this?"

"I thought perhaps you could tell me."

Harry knows the jig is up. No sense denying it.

"I didn't think you'd help me without a little creative inspiration."

"So this whole thing about Chase and his mother and my being his father is all bull shit."

"Not necessarily. He told me the story and swears it's true. I just added the note to give it a touch of authenticity."

"I knew I shouldn't have listened to you. I knew it was a mistake. God damn it!"

Harry signals a waiter and orders a beer.

"Una caña, por favor. You want anything?"

"No. I can't believe this. How could I have been so fucking stupid?"

"Easy: you're still holding onto the past. You know it and I suspected as much. So it wasn't all that difficult talking you into coming with me."

"Harry, shut up!"

"More bad news, I'm afraid. No golf course."

"What?"

"Not even a miniature. Closest one is Santander."

"So there is absolutely no reason for our being here."

"It would appear so, yes. Odd. I really felt we were close this time. I was sure I felt his presence."

RJ just shakes his head: he can't believe this.

About this same time in New York Forrester is seated behind his desk while Dixie paces.

"Try to understand the network's position, Dixie, please. It's not the money…"

"Don't! Do not give me the "It's the principle" speech. "We don't negotiate with terrorists." What crap! I want two million dollars cash right now."

"I've talked to the president of the company and he held an emergency board meeting. They are still adamant: no deal."

"Jesus H. Christ! You're all a bunch of fucking blockheads!"

"Let's say we came up with the money and what we did leaked to the press, which it surely would. How would we look? Where would it end? No journalist on the planet would be safe."

"I don't suppose the ratings have anything to do with that decision, do they. Your new guy is doing very well. Going to be hard putting old Jordan back on the air isn't it."

"Come on, Dixie, that's not fair. You know this decision by the board has nothing to do…"

"I don't give a good goddamn about the "board.""

"Listen, I overheard a conversation last night Bobby was having in his room with a friend of his. They were talking about going to Mexico and buying enough cocaine to bring back here and sell in order to buy back his father. Scared me half to death. But, you know what, he's at least trying to do something, which is more than I can say for you and the fucking board."

Dixie heads for the door.

"Where are you going?"

"Where the fuck do you think I'm going? To get the money. Sell the house. Stocks. The boat. Something. I've only got one more day. One!"

She exits leaving the door open behind her.

Meanwhile back to Jordan and his hosts where a small party in the kitchen is in progress. A soccer game is on the television set. There are ten or so men in the room. No women. Jordan is seated in a straight back chair in the middle of the room. His arms are bound, but loosely so that he can move them, but not loose enough that he could remove a large bandanna that covers his eyes. Hillario, or whatever his name is, is cooking steaks on the grill. Lots of smoke. Another man is playing a flamenco guitar. Several others are clapping their hands in accompaniment. One of the men sings a jota. The food is placed on the table and Jordan's chair is lifted by two large men and placed at the head. A knife and fork are placed in his hands. He doesn't eat.

"Jordano, eat. Pour him some wine. Rosado from Navarra, Jordan. Good stuff. The guy who is loaning us this house has an excellent cellar. Good thing he don't show up … then we would have another guest."

The other men think this is a big joke.

"How is this hombre going to entertain us?"

"You hear that, Jordan? You going to sing us a song?"

"Jordan is still holds knife and fork, but he is defiantly not eating."

"I don't sing and I don't play an instrument."

"Well you got to do something. That's the rule. Got to sing for your supper."

Jordan flexes his jaw muscles, and then seems to relax a bit.

"I'll tell you a joke. Two actors are walking down Sunset Boulevard in Hollywood. They notice a man walking toward them who is wearing a toupee. After the man has passed them one of the actor's says, "Was that guy wearing a toupee?" And the other actor says, "Are you kidding I could fly to Baghdad on that rug.""

The men at the table stare at Jordan in stunned silence. Finally Hillario starts to laugh uproariously and eventually the others follow the bosses lead though it is obvious from the looks on their faces they don't get the joke. Jordan thinking he's a hit smiles and starts to eat.

Dixie is seated in an office across from Warren Small a banker type in his early sixties who is Jordan and Dixie's financial advisor and investor.

I understand, Dixie, believe me. We can do it. It's not going to be easy and it's anything but legal. But, as you say, there appears to be no other choice.

"What do you mean 'anything but legal?'"

"Strictly speaking you must report any large amount of money that you are taking out of the country."

"But I'm not taking it. I'm giving it to someone here."

"Yes, well be that as it may, let's hope we never have to explain it. So, it's essential we keep this to ourselves."

"Have you heard from these people lately?"

"They called the hotel last night to see how I was doing. About getting the money, that is."

"Well, give me the rest of the day. Will you be in this evening?"

"Yes, at the hotel. We have until tomorrow. After that..."

She gets up and he escorts her to the door and kisses her cheek.

"Dixie, I know it's very difficult but try not to worry. We'll work this out."

She leaves and Small returns to his desk where he dials a phone number. While it is ringing he takes the portable handset and walks to the window where he looks out.

"Lieutenant Carter, please. Warren Small calling. He'll know what it's about."

He listens for a moment and then says, "Yes, Lieutenant, she just left. I ... Hello? Hello."

Realizing he has been cut off he turns back to his desk to see Dixie standing there with her finger on the base of the telephone.

"You bastard. "Keep this to ourselves?" You lying, miserable, son of a bitch."

206

She picks up the base of the phone, throws it at him hitting him on the arm and storms out of his office. Small runs after her nursing his arm in the process. He follows her through his reception area where two businessmen are waiting for him. His secretary senses she screwed up.

"She said she left her glasses. Mr. Small?"

He follows Dixie to the elevator where he catches up with her.

"Dixie, I'm sorry. I made a mistake. Please, come back to my office. Let me explain. I know what to do. I'll get the money and I won't speak to the police again, I promise."

Dixie wants to be convinced. To whom else can she turn?

A lovely star strewn night in Mundaka. A slight breeze moves in from the ocean. Harry is walking along the path leading from the old church. He's is smoking a cigar and seems pensive. It is very late. The village is closed for the night. The only movement is from a pair of fishing boats far out to sea. Harry senses something and turns around. Nothing there except a large tree. The church bell rings one solitary time. Harry continues on his walk when suddenly a cord is around his neck, and a knee is pressed into his back. Harry can't get his fingers under the cord. He thrashes violently to one side causing him and his assailant to crash to the ground. The cord is still tightly around his neck and he is losing conscious ness, but not before he grasps the still lit cigar and grinds it into the assailant's hand causing him to cry out in pain and release the rope. In desperation Harry swings a backhanded elbow chop hitting the attacker in the jaw. It is enough to foil the attack and the mugger beats a hasty retreat. Harry catches his breath and looks around the area, but the would-be killer has flown.

The next morning RJ and Harry are sitting at a table talking to police officer Camarena the cop they met earlier in Marbella. In the background a police investigative unit is combing the area where Harry was attacked. Harry is holding ice wrapped in a plastic bag and a towel on his neck.

"I don't understand what you're doing here. Where are the local police?"

"I was in my home office in San Sebastian and was informed of your telephone call to the Guardia Seville. All attacks of this nature are immediately forwarded to me."

Looking at the cordoned off crime scene RJ says, "Do you think they'll find anything?"

"It's possible. Unlike all the other attacks your friend came out alive. Who knows, the man may have dropped something. We'll know soon enough. How are you feeling now?"

"I'm all right. It's a little hard to talk. Other than that I'm just very happy to be alive. What about his hand? He must have a burn mark."

"If we had a suspect and he had a scared hand and you could identify him we would definitely have something, but you said you really didn't get a good look at him."

"That's right. All I know is that he wasn't very tall but was very strong. He might have had blond hair. Hard to tell. He was wearing a dark cap of some kind. Not much of a description, I'm afraid."

"The question remains why you?"

Harry knew this would be coming, but it's still a difficult moment. The time when being a homosexual in

Spain was almost a capital offense is not all that long ago.

"I'm a homosexual."

"I see."

Camarena contemplates this news for a moment his eyes never leaving Harry's.

"But, why you and not your lover?"

"He's not my lover and he's straight. We're friends, that's all."

Camarena appears skeptical.

"You don't believe me do you?"

"RJ, do you see the irony in all this? I spend my entire adult life hiding what I am and now I can't convince a cop I'm queer and you're not?"

"I'm sorry. I was being terribly insensitive. These old habits we have sometimes take a while to change. I believe you. Both of you. In addition, it doesn't make a difference to me one way or the other. But, tell me, this person you look for, he too is a homosexual, no?"

RJ starts to answer. Harry cuts him off.

"Don't answer that. I thought this kind of questioning went out with Franco. What difference does it make anyway?"

"I am sorry, once again and you are absolutely correct. Please accept my apologies. But, I have to ask. All the victims have been homosexual. Somehow there is a connection."

Camarena appears embarrassed and gets up from the table.

"Well, I must get back to the…"

He starts to leave, but doesn't.

"I want to tell you something. It has nothing to do with the attack. My son… he…"

He can't continue and, with a motion of helplessness with his hands, walks away.

"What do you suppose that was all about?"

"I haven't the foggiest. You don't suppose his son is one of the victims."

"I have no idea."

They both watch Camarena approaching a group of other police. He makes a motion toward RJ and Harry.

"So, hombre, tell me."

"Tell you what?"

"Harry…"

"I'm telling you the truth. I couldn't tell if it was Chase."

"You lived with this man. You've slept with him, done god knows what else with him and you expect me to believe you don't know if it was Chase that tried to kill you."

Harry remains silent. He fiddles with the ice pack.

"Let's take a little walk."

They head in the opposite direction from the investigation. Camarena sees them leave but does nothing.

They walk toward the estuary where there are a number of surfers in the water three or five hundred yards away.

"Just before he disappeared … left … we had an argument. He said he wasn't sure about his … choice … what is it they call it in the states … his 'sexual orientation?' He told me he'd been giving it a lot of thought. I took it as a rebuke. We were at our club. I'd had a lot to drink. I guess I knew something was in the wind. I accused him of lying. Said he was queer as queer could be. Called him a faggot. Got really nasty. I was convinced there was another man. Then I tried to hit him. I missed him by a country mile. The next thing I knew I was in the swimming pool and he was holding my head underwater. We'd caused quite a row and evidently some of the quests of the hotel pulled him off me. I passed out and the next morning he was gone."

"And you haven't heard from him since?"

"Not a word."

RJ thinks about all this for a moment as they continue walking.

"What about the hotel, club, whatever it is you call it? What happens to it?"

"Ah, well there's the rub. It's in both our names. We bought it, of course, with money Chase had inherited from your ex-wife, his mother. So he was able to say who got what. If I die before he does, a likely scenario considering the age difference, my half goes to Chase. Should he die first his half goes to you, as does my remaining half upon my death."

"To me? Why? I don't get it."

"Ask him."

"Right. Hand me the phone."

"I think it has to do with guilt on the one hand for trying to frame you for the death of his mother and remorse on the other for never having known you as a father. His way of saying he was sorry. Who can say for sure?"

They both stare out at the surfers in the water and the fishing boats that are near them. Harry takes a cigar out of his pocket … contemplates it for a moment and puts it back.

"Might need this."

A grassy plain across the estuary from Mundaka.

Jordan, Hillario, and the large guard are standing looking at the water a quarter of a mile away. Jordan's hands are loosely tied behind him, no bindings on his legs and he still has on the blindfold.

Hillario says, "So many hills. So many trees. A man could hide here forever and never be found."

"You must be aware that I might be able to identify this place."

"This place, yes. But, the house where you were staying is not near here. Besides, it won't make any difference."

"Because you're going to kill me."

"No, because we're leaving. We only borrowed la casa for a little while. The man who owns it lives in Argentina. He only comes here July and August. We'll clean up. Leave it better than when we arrived. We may even replace his wine. Ha! Maybe not."

Jordan near panic-stricken speaks…almost moans with fear. "I don't believe you. You're going to kill me. I know you are."

He tries to run. The guard holds tight to his leash.

"Calm down. Killing you was never an option. We only told you that to frighten you. A controlling device. Besides, we got what we wanted, thanks to your wife or your company. Who knows? The important thing is we have the money nicely put away in an untraceable Swiss bank account. So clever those Swiss guys. Killing you would only create many, many difficulties. Besides, we're not murderers, we're cooks."

Jordan does not appear to be convinced.

"You know you got everything all screwed up. I watched that documentary the other night about you and your friend el Presidente. He is a good guy. No scandals. Works hard. You? You're another thing. You got this tough guy thing … go anywhere … kill the competition. Got to get that story first. Got to get those ratings. A 'driven man' they called you. Where you driving to driven man?" Jordan is forced to listen to this. He seems to be calming down.

"And you got a lovely wife who must love you even with all the fooling around you do. How come, I wonder? She must be a saint. I saw your little girlfriend on TV last night. She's back in the states. The guy doing the interview called her an 'intern." That's pretty funny, no? Like 'actress' or what's that other one … 'starlet.'"

This is having an effect on Jordan whether he likes it or not.

"So you're going home to your wife and your family and your friend the President. Play some golf. Screw some more young girls. You're a little less rich, perhaps, but you can make that up … if you still have a job."

Later that same day just before sunset RJ and Harry are loading RJ's luggage into a taxi in front of the Hotel La Puerta.

"Keep the car as long as you like, Harry. Within reason, that is. Just try to drop it off in Madrid at the airport when you leave. Well, good luck, Harry. I hope you find him. Send me a postcard."

"I wish you'd stay a little longer. I really feel we're close this time."

"I can't, Harry. I've got to get back. I've got a business to run. A life to live. And if truth be told I'm worn out. The last few days I've been asking myself what the hell I'm doing here anyway and it may be that the answer is that I've not really been looking for Chase at all. Is it really important at this stage in our lives whether or not he's my son? Hard to say. But what I think I've really been doing is looking for answers to the same old questions I've been asking myself for years: is it just a coincidence that my daughter and my ex-wife both died in the same swimming pool and that there were no witnesses? No one saw a thing? And the big question: what was my part in this whole … whatever it was? What could I have done differently that might have saved my daughter's life? And after all these years I'm no closer to finding answers to those questions than you are to finding your friend. You were right, you know, Harry, eventually I've got to quit chasing the past. It's time to move on."

"RJ, is that another Chase pun?" (They both laugh.) "Wait! I just remembered something. Madrid. Chase said someday he wanted to play the course Bing Crosby loves. Chase is crazy about that guy. That's in Madrid. That's where he is. I'll bet on it. We've got to...."

"Harry ... I'm going home.

They both realize it's true.

"I understand. Well, good-bye then. I don't suppose we'll be seeing each other again."

"Knowing you, I wouldn't bet on it."

RJ reaches for the cab door.

"Be careful, Harry. You never know..."

It's not him. I just know it isn't him. RJ, what do I say to him when I find him?

RJ thinks about this for a second.

"You'll think of something."

RJ looks at Harry as if really seeing him for the first time.

"Tell him ... tell him about your father. Tell him you missed him. Tell him you love him. And if you find him...ask him to call me or better yet come and see me. I think we have a lot to talk about."

RJ and Harry hug each other. RJ gets into the cab.

"RJ, I hope you don't think it was all a big waste of time."

RJ thinks about this for a second.

"You know, Harry, you're a lot like Spain: hard, tough, difficult, but, ultimately, worth the struggle."

RJ gets into the cab and sticks his head out the window.

"Wouldn't have missed it for the world."

RJ taps the car driver on the shoulder signaling him to move out.

From high above the town the cab moves along the small road along the beach where the hard-core surfers are still riding the last waves of the day. Had he not totally been lost in his thoughts and had he not been misty eyed RJ might have seen two young men waiting for the next big one. The men are very handsome, tanned, and they are both blond. They laugh about something and it seems they share something more than just a surfing camaraderie. They are lying on their boards faced into the oncoming waves. One of the men is Chase. The other could almost be his double. They are dressed in similar rubber suits. The only difference is that the 'other man' has a cord running from his board to his ankle. It is multi-colored and has a series of knots in it.

And at this very moment not far away high up in the hills he might also have seen a solitary figure with a black hood over his head struggling with a loosely tied binding around his wrists to which he eventually manages to free himself. He then removes the hood. He nervously looks around. No-one. He is quite alone.

And so we are back at the flashy restaurant we first visited in beginning of this story. Jordan's has lost his position as the network's star prime time anchor having been replaced by Tom Kelley the very cute boy wonder who substituted for him while he was being held captive in Spain. Oh, those demographics. Having chosen to accept the retirement package offered by the network Jordan is now officially unemployed.

As you may recall Jordan believes he may have recognized one of his captors who is now one of the restaurants cooks. Jordan is sitting by himself having sent wife Dixie to the ladies room knowing the man will take a close look at this lovely woman as she passes by the open kitchen. When she returns from the ladies room she asks, "Well, is it him?"

Jordan ponders this for a moment.

"No. I was mistaken. Just a guy with a similar mustache. Hillario was smaller. Not him."

Dixie smiles at him. An all-knowing smile.

"Come on. It's him isn't it?"

"Actually, I'm not sure. I only saw his face, actually just one of his eyes, a bit of his face, some facial hair and only once, briefly, through a small crack in a boarded up window and he was back lit. To be sure I'd have to talk to him. I'd know his voice. His laugh for sure. And what if it is him … then what?"

Dixie thinks about this for a bit.

"You call the police. Have him arrested. Or you could ask him for a lion's share of the profits. After all, you paid for this place."

"And if he turns out not to be the right guy, what then? Get sued for making a false accusation? You ready to go?"

"Whenever you are."

She takes a final sip of water.

"Dix, have I changed all that much?"

"From the way you were before the … incident?"

"Dixie looks lovingly at Jordan."

"I have so many answers to that question. Yes, I hope so. You seem different. Softer. You listen to me more attentively… a definite improvement. There are times when you seem to be very far away. Where do you go?"

"A dark room somewhere. A grassy slope overlooking water. And that's about it. Not knowing if I was going to live or die. Whether I'd ever see you or Bobby again. Sometimes I think my mind is trying very hard not to remember. Odd."

"You know going back to your asking me if you've changed. I think, ultimately, the answer to that question can only be answered by you."

"I suppose you're right. I'll think about it … call you when I work it out."

"Or send me a memo?"

"Depends on the answer. Then if I change my mind I can ask you not to read it."

They both laugh at this.

As they are about to stand a man approaches their table. It's Harry.

"Mister and Mrs. Christopher, may I introduce myself? I'm Neville Churchill. I'm with the establishment. Sort of a majordomo, as it were. Just wanted to see how you have enjoyed your repast."

"Please, sit down. Join us, Jordan says."

"Thank you. Is this your first time in Spain Mrs. Christopher?"

"No, I spent a year in Barcelona when I was a student."

"And you Mister Christopher is this the first you've been back since…the, ah…"

"Incident?"

"Yes."

"As a matter of fact it is. Under markedly different circumstances."

"Yes, indeed. Well, nice meeting you both. Please come again and feel free to call on me if there is anything I can do to facilitate your stay in the area."

"Harry hands Jordan his card leaves."

They get up. Jordan leaves cash for the bill and they head for the entrance. As they do Jordan and the chef exchange a very brief glance. Jordan makes no sign that he recognizes him.

Outside the restaurant a parking attendant approaches. It is Chase.

"How was everything, Mr. Jordan?"

"Fine. Just fine, thank you. Sounds like an American accent."

"You got me. Born in Colorado. Spent most of my life in Florida."

"You ever get back?"

"Not in a long time. Going back at Christmas time to see my dad."

Dixie says, "Well, that's nice."

"Yeah, well maybe. Come back and see us."

As they are driving away Jordan says sotto voce, I don't think so.

"What's that, dear?"

"Nothing. Just mumbling to myself."

"That's one way you've changed. You're doing that a lot lately."

THE END

Author's note: ON SUCH A NIGHT AS THIS. Music by Hugh Martin. Lyrics by Marshall Barer.